ANIMALIA PARAL

ANIMALIA PARADOXA
BY HENRIETTA ROSE-INNES

BOILER HOUSE PRESS

Animalia Paradoxa: the taxonomic category created by Carl Linnaeus for mythical, dubious and imaginary animals. They feature in editions 1 – 5 of Linnaeus's *Systema Naturae*, but were removed from subsequent editions.

SANCTUARY

I used to drive that long road with my parents, when they were alive. We had a secret place we went to camp, and after their death I tried to go back every year or two. It never felt dangerous to be alone there, so isolated – who'd know I was there? Of course, the trip had its worries. If I broke down, it might be a long time before anyone passed by.

On that road, fences are the only things standing proud of the earth. I mean the wire sheep-fences, held up by wooden posts and anchored by stones dragged from the fields. They have some power. In the old days, they put a stop to the springbok migrations, when those great wild herds still existed. It's all sheep now, and not too many of them on this dry soil. Still, the livestock is worth something, and so: hundreds of kilometres of wire, pegging out squares, rhombuses, huge dusty parallelograms, the greater geometry only discernible to gods in the hot blue sky.

The gravel road penetrates by means of gates; each fence-crossing must be stopped for, negotiated. Some are marked with rough hand-lettered signs – *maak hek toe* – but generally the importance of closing these gates is understood. Each one is a test. Every farmer has his way, his own cobbled-together trademark technique for keeping the gate latched. A mechanism too clever for sheep, not too clever for the rare human visitor. Some are pins and some are chains, some hooks and some shackles. Some are sturdily home-engineered from sections of pipe, some just twists of rusty wire. Once you've passed through five or six of these variants, you grow more fluent in the language of latch and hasp; but still, it is a tedious business, the opening and the closing. It's better to have someone along with you, on gate duty. When I used to travel with my parents, I was always the one to nip out, feet hurting on the hot stones, and wrestle with the bolts.

On this particular trip, I was feeling more anxious than usual, perhaps because the car had been acting up, starting unwillingly. I left the engine running as I worked the gates, just in case. After passing through each one, I felt momentary paranoia, the urge to go back and check that I'd closed it properly. I imagined sheep streaming through; consequences. But the further I went the harder it seemed to turn around. The thought of latching and unlatching all those farm gates in reverse was exhausting. And so I continued, locking myself deeper and deeper into the countryside.

Although it came as a surprise, I was actually glad to see another vehicle. At first it was just a cloud of orange dust, clarifying to show the boxy shape of a large new four-by-four, halted ahead of me. A woman hopped out of the passenger seat to deal with the gate. I was annoyed that she closed it behind them: it meant a double trip for me, to fiddle with the thing both before and after driving through. But by the next gate, the woman had noticed me, and after that she left the gate open at each stop. She was a big woman, but moving quickly, as if harried. Each time, she turned her head to stare – seemed almost to be seeking out my eyes – and then turned quickly back, as if something tugged at her from inside the car. She hurried to drag the long metal gate through its arc in the dust. The driver waited for her quite far down the road, further than was necessary. She had to trot to catch up, and the car started rolling forward almost before she had the door closed. I couldn't see much through the dust-caked rear window, but I could tell that a bully was in the driver's seat.

By the sixth or seventh gate, things had escalated. The woman was left behind, clutching the top bar of the gate as the vehicle roared away. I drove through cautiously, then stopped and opened my passenger door. The woman closed the gate behind us. By now, the four-by-four was receding into the dust ahead.

Lowering herself into the car seat, she didn't bother with a smile.

'Thank you,' she said, pulling the door shut.

'Are you all right?' I asked.

She nodded tightly. She wore a khaki blouse and slacks. Her large cheeks would be sheened with sweat if they weren't powdered matte with orange dust.

'He's just in a mood,' she said. 'They'll be up ahead.' She pressed her curly, sweat-darkened hair back with her palms, leaving streaks on her temples. She had rather large, staring eyes: I could see only the right-hand one, from the side, as she kept it fixed on the road ahead.

Five minutes later, we came upon the next gate. The four-by-four was crouched there, waiting. We pulled up behind. The woman let herself out with another stiff thank-you and went to open the gate for him as before. On the other side, she climbed back into their car as if nothing had happened. Now I could see the tops of small heads in the back seat. The air inside my car crackled with the tension and unhappiness of the departed woman. She'd left a patch of dust on the passenger seat, a handprint clamped to the door handle.

There were no more gates. The four-by-four took a turn to the left, onto the tarred driveway of a new nature reserve. It was a fancy place, the first on this road with a high game fence. The entrance was marked by an arch made of two cement elephant tusks curving into the sky, although there were no longer any elephants in this part of the world. *Khaya Leone Lion Sanctuary*, said a sign below, faux-carved into faux-ivory.

I carried on along the gravel road, now fenced on one side by the gleaming grid of the two-metre game fence. After a few kilometres the fence turned a corner and marched away into the landscape, dead straight, leaving me alone with the road again.

My turn-off, a narrow track not wide enough for two cars, was easier to spot than I'd feared. As soon as I'd taken it I felt better: less observed, more securely alone. I'd made good time and it was still afternoon. I found the old campsite without trouble, and it was the same as ever. The still, cool air under the thorn trees, the white sand, the ruin of an old mud-wall homestead with owls and doves in its eaves and the bones of a sheep, bleached white, inside next to the fireplace. Nothing changed here except the incremental operations of nature at its quietest: the slow expansion of a wasp nest, a fallen tree surrendering to humus. New-hatched spiders spinning old patterns. And above all, the river. Such a surprise, the sudden moistening and cooling as you picked your way down the bank; the luxurious sweep of shining slate-coloured water glimpsed through the branches.

Here the river was quite deep and smooth. Upstream, to the left, it cut into the land that had seemed so flat from the road, opening up a rocky passage, with little rapids, a modest ravine, a series of miniature cliffs.

I took my shoes off and felt the mud on my feet, pursuing the pleasure of the cool water as it inched up my calves. I hadn't realised how parched I'd been. I stripped down to my bra and panties and paddled out, losing the river bottom at times. The current was very slow, barely noticeable, and it was easy to wade upstream, swimming through the deeper spots, occasionally hurting my feet where the water rushed white over the stony bed. I sang to myself: old campfire songs.

But on the opposite bank, something new. A game fence came down to the water to drink, taut and shining. A board attached to it said, *Khaya Leone, Trespassers will be Prosecuted*. And beyond that, just around the bend, stood a big house built of raw-looking red wood, low-slung and modern, with a deck stretching out over the water. There was no sign of life – the curtains were drawn – but I doggy-paddled quickly past, putting the house behind me and out of sight. I crossed over some rocks where the water grew shallow, and waded upstream until I felt the solitude seal around me again. Still, something was spoilt.

I rested on a rock for a while like a crocodile, and then, as the sun moved down the sky, began to drift back downstream. Three blond children stood in the shallows, their bright heads bent over the stream. They were laughing and tossing stones into the deeper pools, skipping them with practised gestures. The oldest boy made one zing from his snapped finger with a noise like a bumblebee. I looked around for the parents, because these three boys were very young to be here by themselves – the oldest nine or ten, the others younger still. When they saw me they stopped smiling and stood straight, in a row. Made shy by their identical stares, I tried to keep my underwear submerged, scampering awkwardly over the exposed stones and plunging back into the waist-deep water. I smiled at them gamely and the smallest – not more than five years old – raised a hand.

Still, it was nice to see children so free, I thought. Barefoot boys, their soles tough enough not to flinch on the pebbles. Suburban children would be shoed and daubed in sunscreen and never allowed out by themselves in the first place.

As I floated around the next bend I noticed a familiar vehicle in the car port of the wooden house. The big curly-haired woman was sitting on the deck, her pants rolled to the knee and her feet in the stream. Like her sons she gave me an unsmiling look, a hesitant wave. A man – her husband, must be – was sitting further back in the shade of the patio, a beer on the ground next to his camp chair. I was surprised to see a rifle laid across his knees, but then I realised: Khaya Leone was probably one of those places people came to hunt. Canned lions, maybe. I floated on past, feeling even less inclined to like the family.

As I pulled myself out of the water and walked back to my camp, my feet prickling in the thorny ground, I was angry. They were so close by, these people; they might not see my campsite, but my sense of boundless isolation was gone. Maybe I should just leave again, despite the long way I'd driven. Not tonight, but first thing tomorrow.

After the sun set I went up the low koppie behind the ruined house and looked down on the opposite shore. The wooden house was right there, very close, paraffin lamps lit on the patio. The man was poking coals in the braai and drinking another beer, but the woman and children were out of sight. He was a rangy, tanned man, his face darkened by stubble. When he lifted his head, alert and listening, I felt myself go rigid like a wild creature in hiding. He called into the house, and I backed down the hillside before the woman could come out. I was sure her curious, somehow beseeching gaze would find me out.

That night I laid out my sleeping bag in the sand as we always used to do, but things were different, wrong: tiny insects feasted on my face and my feet, and the sleeping bag was too hot to zip up. All night I heard new things; not just the ticking of the cooling earth, not just the calls of night birds, but ambiguous, threatening sounds. They might just have been the conversation of water and frogs, but in my half-dreaming, itching state they could also be footsteps, scheming human speech, and at one point something that sounded like roaring. I must have drowsed off, because some sharp rupture jerked me awake in the early-morning hours, and for a panicked moment I knew something big and malevolent was thrashing up through the river reeds. Lions can't swim, I told myself, and fell back into an uneasy sleep.

In the early morning, the boys were standing there at the edge of my campsite, three in a row, barefoot, wearing only underpants. I thought perhaps it was some kind of game they were playing, repaying my visit to their side of the river. But then I saw the tight jaw of the oldest child, and that the two youngest were clutching each others' hands. They must have waded across at the shallow part of the river. It would not have been so shallow for the littlest boy, who looked soaked from head to toe, his hair slicked back against his small skull. They were wiry kids, narrow-hipped, long-legged and knob-kneed, not frail but with no flesh to spare. Their little-boy underpants, damp, clung to their groins. I noticed a blue bruise on the oldest boy's ribcage. More than anything they looked cold. I wanted to cover them in blankets, wrap them in towels.

'What's happened?' I asked.

The oldest boy had clamped his mouth so tight I imagined I could hear his milky teeth grinding in his mouth. The smallest boy started crying. The middle child opened his mouth and the freed voice came out in a shout: 'It was a *lion!*' Then he started to cry too, and the youngest gave a whoop of caught breath and began to howl even harder.

The older boy came forward, as if to speak to me confidentially, but he had no control of his voice either. 'Our Ma said we must come across,' he said, too loud. 'Pa got hurt.'

'By a *lion!*'

The fright came through me in a cold ripple. 'Get in the car,' I said.

They obeyed me quickly, with what seemed like relief. I opened the car and then locked them in, all three in the back seat. These children seemed accustomed to silent compliance.

'Stay here, ok? Sit tight.'

The oldest nodded, voice gone again.

Out of the boot I fetched a water bottle, a chocolate bar and some oranges, the few spare t-shirts and towels I had. I opened the car and passed the stuff back to the boys, then cracked the window down a bit – thinking of overheated dogs in cars – and closed the door and locked it. On second thoughts I tossed the keys through to the back seat.

'Keep inside, ok? Keep it locked.'

Nods.

'Your father, does he need an ambulance? Is your mom ok? Your ma?'

The boys looked frightened. The littlest bit down on an orange.

I went back to the river and it seemed deeper, much too deep for such young kids to have attempted it. The water was still dark in the morning shade, and felt silky and some-how thick against my skin as I went in: harder to push aside, the current more insistent. When I came around the bend I swam across the width of the stream and pulled myself up onto the wooden deck of the house, and crouched there for a moment, listening. No sound except a small bird piping, somewhere off in the bush.

Inside, it was too neat for a holiday house. I looked into each room in turn, seeing folded towels, stacked plates. Nothing was disturbed, nothing out of place. I felt strange and wild here, tracking river mud across the swept floor-boards. I went through the back door into the vehicle bay, checking the empty seats of the four-by-four. The light was brighter out back.

Behind the carport was a row of casuarinas, shedding their messy needles, and beyond that I found myself in a dry field, cultivated once but now given over to small tough succulents, sharp red-brown pebbles and patches of shattered stone pavement. I was barefoot but I barely felt the thorns. The field was empty, but halfway across it was a pile of large stones, probably hauled there when the farmer first cleared the field. Beyond the field I could see the grid of the game fence, its top edge glinting in the new sun. I sniffed the air. How bright the tiny flowers, white and yellow; but there was a tang of something else, sharp and dirty, running like a wire through the blue air.

Something was wrong with that pile of stones. A grey, blunt point sticking out from behind it at ground level. The stones were piled maybe a metre high: high enough to hide any scene I might imagine, however gruesome. Even the long, crouched body of a lioness. With each step I took forward, the greyish nub became clearer, more comprehensible. It turned into the toe of a shoe. A running shoe. I could see a white sock. A hairy ankle.

I stood quite still for long time, trembling lightly, watching that foot in its shoe. It did not move. I tried to feel on my skin if there was a slight breeze, and which way it was carrying my scent. Altering the angle of my approach, I came silently over the stones, first climbing and then creeping, pressing my belly to the warming curve of the topmost rock. Moving forward in millimetres, I peered over, and down.

Very close to my eyes was the man's forehead. He was sitting against the rocks, and his red-burned face was turned up to mine, the jaw slack to show the grey teeth of his lower jaw. In the centre of his forehead was a clean red hole. A red line ran down from it into his eye. The lion's tooth, was my first thought. I looked into his drying blue eye.

The backs of my knees start to prickle from the sun, and a small black lizard crept out and over the back of my hand and vanished into a crack in the stone. Quietly, so as not to disturb the lizard or any other creature, I lowered myself down from the pile of rocks and stepped carefully back though the grass towards the house. I walked along the row of trees but there was no sign of the woman in their meagre shade. Perhaps I should call out for the wife, make some kind of noise, but I knew there would be no sound coming from my chest. My jaws were clamped tight shut. Then I remembered about the children.

The swim back across the river was hard, wearying; my muscles were tired. Perhaps I had just gone back and forth too many times. I felt like one more crossing would sink me.

I didn't have much to pack up: I had barely made camp the night before, just unrolling my sleeping bag on the sand. The interior of my car was hot and filled with the mucous odour of children's distress. The younger children were asleep or pretending to be, but the oldest was wide awake, his knobby knees sticking out from under my too-large T-shirt. I held out my hand for the car keys.

'Did you see it?' he asked.

I didn't know what to say. I shook my head.

'The lion? Did you see it?'

'No, no I didn't see the lion.'

I couldn't drive at first, with the trembling in my hands, so I busied myself by checking that the boys were wrapped in t-shirts and towels, although that was hardly what they needed in the growing heat; that they drank water and passed around the tube of gumdrops from the glove compartment. Then I sat for a moment gripping the key in the ignition, certain it would fail. But the engine turned first try, loud in the clearing.

Disturbed, the resident owl drifted silently from the crumbling window of the mud house, through the morning air and into the trees. As we drove away, our wheels covered the place in dust.

She was standing at the entrance to the game lodge, the absurd tusks casting bars of morning shadow over her face. She held the long gun carelessly in one hand, dragging the butt in the gravel as she came forward to meet us.

'Let's leave that behind, shall we,' I said.

She shrugged, and laid the rifle down on the road next to her.

'They might need it,' she said.

'Who?'

'The police.'

I thought about this. 'Okay. Then put it in the boot. It's open.'

Obedient, she picked the gun up again and went round to the back of the car and laid the gun sideways in the boot, then came back and took her place on the passenger seat.

'Hello Ma,' said the oldest boy, and she looked at him levelly in the rear-view mirror.

'Hello my boy,' she said.

And so we headed back, along the same route as before, with the quiet boys in the back. At one point the eldest stirred and pushed his hand through the gap between the seats to touch his mother's arm. She jumped a little and I realised how much tension was in her slow form. Her arms were folded across her bosom and with just the fingertips of her left hand she trapped the son's fingertips against the flesh of her bicep and held them there.

She was docile. At each farm gate we stopped and she left the car and opened the latch and pulled the long arm of the gate through its arc in the dust. I drove through and waited while she did up the complex metal knot, and then we moved on again, making good our slow, methodical escape. Over and over again we did this, locking ourselves out for good, locking it all away behind us: the owls and the lions, the tiny flowers and the wasps; the sand and the red rocks; the deep, cool river.

THE SECOND LAW

I was in the shop mostly to warm myself – the mall was heated, the weather bitter – but I also had a dumb, nostalgic fondness for places like this. Miniature pool tables, World's Greatest Dad mugs, aprons fitted with plastic boobs. That kind of thing. I was playing with the old-school executive toys, making the spheres of a Newton's cradle clack back and forth, when the store assistant came over.

'Something for your boyfriend?'

Cheeky, I thought. He was a spruce young guy in a royal-blue polo shirt, tucked in to show off a neatly solid chest. *Ryan* was sewn on the breast pocket.

'No boyfriend,' I said.

'No? That's a shame.'

'I need a get-well gift, actually. For my dad, he's been in hospital.' I looked past him at a gadget on the shelf. 'What's that?'

A Perspex wheel the size of a saucer was mounted upright on a metal stand. It was hollow, and inside you could see a dozen or so ball bearings, trapped in separate compartments.

'Perpetual motion machine.'

Now I smiled. 'Come on.'

'No seriously, it's the real thing.'

He reached out and spun the wheel. The motion was silky and frictionless; the balls made a controlled clatter as they went around, like a miniature hailstorm. Its cheerful flicker brought back something I hadn't thought about for years: a Christmas ornament my dad made for my mother, with his own hands, a long time ago. Tin angels on a round-about, propelled by the breath of little red candles. Those hot, bright southern Christmases.

'It's actually from an original design by Leonardo da Vinci,' Ryan was saying. 'See, the balls get carried up to the top, and then their weight pulls the wheel around again, and it just carries on and on. Perfect system.'

I let him talk. Leonardo. Momentum, action, reaction. Energy something something. I hadn't been in the UK long, and the accent in this town escaped me at times. Words got lost, especially when people spoke fast, and also when they were talking rubbish. Nice hair, though, I thought: coppery, razored at the sides and gelled in the front. Soft gold on the backs of his fingers. The guy was in good condi-tion – no chips or scuffs, white teeth, bright eyes. He stood close enough for me to catch his warmth, and his citrus aftershave.

'See?'

'It's clever, sure.'

'And it goes forever,' he said with a wink.

It was a good one, as winks go. A little voltage passed

between us, and something started up inside me in response: a flywheel, a spinning top.

It didn't last. As I headed home with my plastic carrier bag, the buzz of the shop bled away and the town set coldly around me. It was one of those white-skied, soundless days, everything still and empty, no one on the streets or at the windows. It felt like I was the one moving thing in a winter painting; or as if the locals had gathered in a crowd some streets away and were standing there in silence, listening to my footsteps, waiting for me to pass.

Back at the flat, I checked my emails. There was an update from the home carer, Yolisa. Dad was out of hospital, she wrote, in her calm, direct way, but frail and sleeping much of the time. Dad liked Yolisa; we'd employed her to nurse him several times before. She was a driven twenty-something, pulling night shifts and studying by correspondence in the hopes of getting into medical school. I often wondered what she thought of me and Martin, so far away, when surely our father needed us there. I wrote back to tell her that my brother was on his way.

Martin Skyped me that evening from some alien time zone, a stopover on a crooked path from Vancouver to Cape Town – tickets purchased last-minute, flights zigzagging east and south and west and south again. I was lying on the couch wrapped in a duvet, laptop held up so that my brother's face floated above mine. Behind him, a tall viewing window was filled with that melancholy departure-lounge light I knew too well, the runway sun perpetually setting. Airside time. Over his shoulder I could see a tiny aeroplane in peach-coloured space, catching a spark.

'Is it late?' he asked. 'Did I wake you?'

'It's fine.'

Time differences: we were always getting them wrong, mixing up a.m. and p.m., adding three hours instead of subtracting seven, or whatever. You lose track. Martin lived in Canada and we both travelled a lot, two roving corners of a triangle, with Dad back in South Africa the one fixed point. Between us, in the last eighteen months we could count off Indonesia, Russia, Japan, Venezuela. At times we were as far from each other as it's possible for three people on planet Earth to be. To calculate the lag before making a call, I always had to close my eyes and picture a globe, then turn it in my mind to make the sun appear on the right and progress to the left, rising and setting on each of us in turn.

'Should I come too?' I asked. 'Maybe I should just get on a plane.'

Nothing really prevented me doing that – I'd finished up on the job that had brought me to this town, fitting out a restaurant – but I had a flight booked to New York in a couple of weeks' time; it would be expensive to change plans.

'Let's see when I get there. How bad it is,' said Martin.

'Your call.'

'My turn.'

This was the drill: we alternated crises. My last trip home had been four months before, when Dad dislocated his shoulder in a fall. This time it seemed worse, some kind of heart failure.

'When will you get there?' I asked.

'Uh, eleven hours? Maybe twelve?'

'Dad would know.'

'To the second.'

I couldn't make out Martin's expression with the light behind him, but his voice was weary and distant. My ears felt blocked and my throat tight, like something was stuck there. Perhaps I was getting sick.

These were the only conversations we had nowadays: medication; complications; insurance; visas. The logistics of keeping a rickety family up and running, across three continents. We were always in transit, voices warped over long-distance lines, connections breaking; faces pallid in airport lounges or reflected in the black windows of night trains. Neither of us had lives that were complicated to step out of for a week or three – single, self-employed – but we were tired, my brother and I. It was taking long years for my father's clock to wind down.

I sound cold, I know. I was. It was my first winter in England, and I was bloody freezing.

'Tell Dad I got him a present,' I said. 'For next time.'

And it seemed like that plane was still hanging there, in just the same place above my brother's left shoulder, catching the last flash of sun.

Nothing to do but wait. I took my boxed-up perpetual-motion machine out of its bag. On the front was Leonardo's sketch of the device, fine arcs of umber ink, with some lines of his mirror writing underneath. I was feeling light-headed and empty, almost weightless, while the box seemed heavier than it ought to be. Inside, the ball bearings, supernaturally dense, vibrated with a desire to move and keep moving. I didn't want to open it up – it was meant for Dad – but my hands were drawn magnetically, were already lifting the flaps.

Inside, there was a leaflet, explaining: Leonardo himself knew that perpetual motion was a myth, that it outraged the laws of physics. Designing these machines was a way of demonstrating their impossibility. *For entertainment and educational purposes only*, the small print emphasised; no claims of inexhaustible energy were made. Screw the laws of physics, I thought. I'd seen the thing work. Overleaf was an exploded diagram which I ignored, having no brain for that kind of thing. How hard could it be to assemble, even for me?

Two halves of the Perspex wheel had to be snapped together and secured with tiny screws. The axle, a steel pin that went through the middle, rested in slots in the metal base. The silver balls came separately, in a plastic packet, and of course I'd forgotten to feed them into their compartments, so was forced to dismantle everything and start again. Eventually I had it set up on the kitchen counter. But when I gave it a turn, the wheel was sluggish, as if the ball bearings had lost their vim. No matter how briskly I snapped it around, after a few revolutions the thing faltered and stopped. No hum, no clatter.

Dad, I thought. I need a hand.

Dad in his workshop under the house, tinkering. It was a serene space, sawdust scattered on the cement floor, bolts and nails gleaming in the lined-up jam-jars. Sparks flew, though, when my father got to work, a big man bearing down with his drill or his soldering iron. An engineer by trade, in his free time he was timber whisperer, clock surgeon, motor magician, always whistling a tune through his teeth. He built our bunk-beds and our radio, he put my first car together from parts and later, when Martin blunderingly drove that same car into the side of the garage, he bricked up the hole and splinted my brother's broken nose himself. He could fix the world.

There was only a year between us, Martin and me. As little kids, we'd often be down there with our dad, messing with wood offcuts and clamps and dead spark plugs. We liked the weights and textures of these things; we used them to play House and Fashion Show and War, and then Dad had to shout at us to clean our mess and put the tools back on their pegboard hooks. We were feckless, dreamy kids, easily bored. As adolescents, we largely retreated to our bedrooms, those less demanding spaces.

Still, we'd ask him for help with things we couldn't do. Dad was patient but unyielding. 'Figure it out,' he'd say when I showed him the electrical diagrams in my grade-eight physics workbook. 'I'm not going to give you the answer. Concentrate. *Look* at it.' Or to Martin, despondently poking at his jammed-up bicycle gears: 'Take your time, don't panic. The answer's right in front of you. Just use your eyes.'

But looking hard at things clarified nothing. Martin's dislocated bike chain and my circuit diagrams were flourishes of the same difficult script, more cryptic than Leonardo's trick writing. It was perhaps the true text of the universe, but one we'd never learn to read.

'You're like your mother, both of you,' Dad conceded. 'She was helluva creative.' She'd up and left when we were very small, too young to really remember. Dad didn't speak about her much, and it was better like that: it was shocking to us, to hear even brief uncertainty or sadness in his voice. 'You get that from her – the artistic side.'

And we did try to make that true. It felt like I was doing it for him, to spare him somehow, when I dropped the science classes and studied art instead. Martin ended up in advertising, and I went into interiors: finding décor for hotels and upmarket restaurants. My trademark pieces were decorative antique mechanisms: clocks, astrolabes and suchlike. High-end steampunk.

We found these jobs easier to do at a distance from Dad's workshop, at the far ends of the world. Our father stayed where he was, growing old. He still cut perfect dovetail joints. Made engines turn.

We came home from time to time. I brought him gifts, usually faux-mechanical trinkets from museum gift-shops and novelty stores. A wind-up robot, a tiny music box with its pretty machinery exposed, a puzzle involving magnets. I worried that they might seem trivial, derisive even, but Dad always glowed with pleasure to receive them. Perhaps he understood that they were gestures, the closest I could get to a shared language.

The webcam showed a bedroom curtained and dim; it might be day or night.

'He's asleep,' Martin said softly, tilting back in the chair to let me see the bed.

There was a body under the sheet, a head sunk in the pillow. The webcam was cheap, and my father's face was indistinct.

'Hi Dad.'

Yolisa was standing in the background, pixelated, busy with pill-bottles. She raised her hand and I returned the salute; it didn't seem right to smile.

Martin leaned in privately, blocking my view. He didn't quite meet my eyes though, in the strange way Skype imposes: that shifty, lowered look.

'Should I come? I can come,' I said. 'I can buy a ticket right now.'

'I don't know. Maybe. The doctor says wait and see.'

'But you'll call me? If anything happens, call me straight away.'

'Of course.'

After he'd logged off, I touched my forehead to the faint warmth of the screen.

At altitude, there'd be tiny shards of ice trapped inside the double window, but on descent they'd melt away. The plexiglass would grow warm and lit. Sunlight on my eyelids and my lips, and below, our shadow falling down the curve of the world, crossing the ghostly latitudes. South. I wanted to be in flight right now; to be converging on the still point where my brother was, where my father lay. Our dad, who in his whole life had never travelled on a plane.

I called up the shop to complain. I recognized Ryan's voice at once, quick and light, although I still couldn't make out everything he said. He was having trouble understanding me too: this knot in my throat made it hard to get the words out.

'Sorry?' I said.

'What?'

'The machine doesn't work,' I repeated.

'No shit? The one here is working fine, it's been going non-stop. Listen.'

I heard footsteps as he crossed the shop, and then a different noise. Through the phone, the wheel's clatter was muted. It sounded like the needle on an old LP, scratching out revolutions after the last song has stopped.

I said, 'Mine doesn't sound like that.'

'Could be you haven't set it up right? You want to bring it in?'

I swallowed. I felt stupidly angry, almost to tears. 'No, not really. That wouldn't be convenient.' And truly, the idea of lugging the thing back through the cold streets was bleak. 'Look ... never mind.'

'Wait, wait.' There was a pause. I knew what was coming. 'I could come over there? Take a look?'

I thought about it for a minute. That background vibration stole into my ears again, and I felt in my chest an answering hum.

'Maybe you should,' I said.

Night passed, then day. I woke at four a.m., fell asleep at noon, woke at six, dreaming through patches of dark and light. My body was unsure where it was, or when, drifting in the slow time of my father's house, where things changed at the pace of a quietening body: tiny collapses and depletions, barely perceptible from hour to hour. Whenever I logged in, either Yolisa or Martin was sitting awake, keeping vigil. On top of the bookshelf next to the bed, along with the meds, I could make out a row of the gadgets I'd got for Dad over the years. Silver balls suspended. A metal stick-figure on a bicycle, balanced on a pin. Nothing moved.

And in the small hours, this wintry vision; Yolisa, upright in the bedside chair, a textbook in her hands, reading aloud. Face lit like the moon by blue computer light, her voice gently chiding: *Every process occurring in nature proceeds in the sense in which the sum of the entropies of all bodies taking part in the process ...*

He never quite woke.

Ryan arrived in the evening, a screwdriver in his top pocket. It was strange to see him in my house, in his bright blue shirt. I showed him the stuck machine.

'Can you get it working?' I asked.

'I can give it a go,' he said.

I made tea for us while he fiddled with the machine on the kitchen counter, unscrewing everything and dismantling it and removing all the balls. Then methodically building it up again. I watched his hands, his precise and measured movements. There was the faintest scent of sawdust in the kitchen. Of sparks off metal. It only took him twenty minutes. Then he folded his arms and gave his work a nod. 'There,' he said. 'You'd done the screws too tight, that's all. Nothing wrong with her.'

'But ...?' The machine looked exactly the same. Gleaming and still.

'It just needs a turn. Look –' And he raised a hand as if to smack it into motion.

I must have made a strange sound, because he stopped, hand in the air. We looked at each other. I wanted to speak, but my throat was swollen up. I touched my neck.

And without hesitation he changed direction, moved his hand to my throat, gentle, thumb resting in the space where my shirt collar fell open. As if he could tell, as if he knew I had something lodged and hurting there. I swallowed, and felt a pop in my ears. Then everything started up again with a rush.

We went upstairs to the cold bed and took off our clothes. His torso was whiter than I'd thought, English pale, and hair dark at the groin. I'd imagined him golden all the way through. Still, his skin was hot and I pushed my chilled self against it, face, breasts, thighs. This was easy, like sitting down hungry to a meal. A simple magic, one I could do, one I was good at, even. Action, reaction. We moved, held still and moved again; and in the held moments – mouth to mouth, hip to hip – I felt the spin inside.

Waking again, in a dark and placeless hour. Up on one elbow, starting the computer. The camera in Dad's room was on but the chair was empty, Yolisa's book splayed on the armrest.

The top half of the bed filled the screen. Dad's head against the pillows was tilted towards me. I could see his face clearly despite the low light, as if the thin air of these small hours had pulled the webcam into focus. Every shadowed dip and ridge, each crease and hollow. The sheet was pulled down, the bones of his shrunken chest exposed. He'd always been such a strong man. On my last visit, he'd let me cut his toenails, holding his ruined feet between my knees. All intimacies allowed.

I watched his chest for movement, and wondered if he was gone; if I was sitting with my father's corpse. But then his eyes came open. Bright points in the dark, each holding a crescent moon of blue reflected light.

I wasn't sure how much he could perceive. If he saw the young man sleeping pressed against my back, arm draped across my breasts. It felt right, though, to lie like that, my father before me, and for us to be watching each other, uncovered and frank. Him in his dying and me in my living, in the midst of life. When does a parent ever have that chance, to see a child so naked; for a child to see a parent so? I looked, and he looked back, half a world apart but together, breathing softly, breathing yet.

I blinked, and he answered: eyes fluttering, shuttering, shut. He seemed to sleep.

After the screen went dark, I turned back into the circle of Ryan's arms. My palm on the sweat-damp base of his spine. My bed smelled of him now, his true body: under the aftershave, salt and sour. We'd worn each other down a little, through to the real skin.

'Are you crying?' he asked.

'No.'

I took his erection in my hand and we started up again. The pleasure was different now, more delicate; it was something we passed between us, balanced on the tips of our fingers and on our tongues, not letting it drop. And it seemed like we could do this forever, falling and catching, light and heavy, the wheel spinning in place and not ever moving forward. As if in this way we could hold back the hours; as if in this way the morning might never come.

But the earth did turn. The sun came up. It was a clear day, too, the first pale warmth of the year.

For long minutes I lay in my childhood bed, a summer day, listening to Dad in his workshop. Taps and knocks and grinds; that breathy whistle as he chivvied some stubborn clockwork child into compliance. But the tune was wrong, not one of my father's. It was a something new off the radio – a song for a young man.

Oh right, I remembered, waking properly. I'm here. It's him.

A few brisk brushing and sorting noises, and then a shipshape silence downstairs. Job done, good to go. I lay still, wondering what came next. If Ryan would come back up the stairs, would fall on me, if we would fall for each other again.

Instead I heard the front door open, then quietly shut. Click of the latch. I breathed.

He'd left something changed, though. The silence was not absolute. There was a silvery whisper, like a tap running, growing more insistent the longer I lay there, until at last I had to stand up and go downstairs to see.

The repaired machine looked like it might take off from the table and hover. It was spinning so fast – the spokes a solid blur – that it might as well have been standing still, but for the ripple of distortion in the sunbeam that fell across it. And that chirring music.

I made myself a cup of coffee. Sat down before the machine. Let my eyes fill with its hiss, let myself get dizzy with it, lose my bearings, the hub a fixed point in a turning world. For a moment my eyes flipped the rotation so the wheel seemed to shiver into reverse, then cycle forwards again.

Stop that, I said to myself. Concentrate. Look, think. Work it out. I'm not going to tell you the answer.

And I did look. I watched the wheel turn until I understood. I saw how one might believe that the balls could fall forever, but that they could not, logically; that drag and friction bleeds the will from any system, in the end. Once I'd thought this through, once I'd got it, I put out my hand to stop the spin.

Silence, immediate and profound. Stillness spread concentrically from the machine: the blood in my hands slowing, the steam ceasing to rise from the coffee mug, the air in the room a held breath, the cars stopped dead on the street outside and every leaf on every tree poised at a precise angle to the sun; the sun itself cooling in its heaven and the planets grinding down, grinding slower, gears disengaging, everything losing power and drifting, drifting to a halt.

And then in the corner of my eye the green light of the computer blinking on, and sound returning, and I guessed that was Martin calling.

PROMENADE

I haven't changed much, over the years. When I look in the mirror, the experience is much the same as it was when I was a younger man. My teeth have not yellowed and my eyesight is remarkably good. Even my finger- and toenails, I suspect, do not edge out from my extremities as rapidly as other people's do. Everyone assumes that I'm in my early forties, when in fact I'm fifty-four – a long way from retirement, but still significantly older than my colleagues at the ad agency. Of course I'm balding now, but even this has helped to freeze me in time. I used to style my hair differently, part it this way and that, grow it and trim it; but I am stuck now with this look, this length: a conservative short cut around the bald spot at the crown. Anything else looks foolish.

It is partially the adipose layer beneath the skin, I believe, that helps to preserve my looks. Slightly plump people, I've often noticed, seem to age better than the bony ones: the skin stays taut for longer, the skeletons submerged. Yes, I am a little overweight, as I have been since my early thirties.

I've tried to lose the excess, but my body remains impervious. A few years back, I put myself through a stern fitness regime – low-fat foods, the gym. There was no observable impact on my weight or muscle tone. I have a metabolism in perfect equilibrium, it seems. Still, I exercise, frequently if moderately. Because what would happen if I stopped?

So it is that every evening after work, at six sharp, I take my promenade along the sea wall near my flat. I clip along at a steady pace: a little more than a walk, a little less than a jog. My fists are bunched before my chest; I thrust them forward and back, kicking my feet one-two one-two, my elbows winging to the sides. Yes, I am one of those speed-walkers. I know it's undignified, but it's the only way to get up any kind of sweat without actually running. I have the gear: special lightweight sweatpants, athletic socks, sweat-wicking tops in the latest high-tech fabrics. (No vests; I really am too old for that.) Once a year I buy a new pair of Nikes or New Balances, a virtuous treat.

On my outward journey, the sea lies to my left, grey or blue or silver. Fifteen minutes at a swift stride from my flat down the steep street, to the sea wall and along the path to the traffic lights opposite the garage and café. Here I pause to stretch on the strip of lawn, before continuing another fifteen minutes along the promenade as far as the public toilets. Then I wheel around and go back in the other direction, one-two one-two, with the sea on my right, half an hour, pausing only to cross at the lights to the café for the day's *Argus*. I roll the newspaper tightly and hold it baton-like in one hand for the rest of the route home (only unsatisfactory on the weekends, when the editions are too fat for comfort). I always take with me just enough change in the special zip-up pocket in my top – plus twenty cents, because sometimes they put up the price without warning – and my house key. No wallet or phone; although the promenade is busy and safe at that time, you can never be too careful. And I like to stay light.

The thing about walking along a sea wall is that your options are limited: you can only go forward or back. You can't head off to the side without falling into the sea, or ploughing across the lawn through the children's swings and roundabouts and into the traffic. The lack of choice is soothing, and I'm quite content to follow my established route, each time the same. It is a beautiful walk, especially on still evenings when the sea is flat and the sky clear, or lightly flecked with peachy clouds. The water glows and swirls like cognac. Everyone I meet, coming or going, is gilded on either the left or right sides of their faces with pink or saffron, and they all seem serene and calm and somehow meditative in the generous light. I know I do.

People comment on that: my serenity. But often I am not calm inside, not at all, especially not in the boiling light of those late evenings. It is a dramatic coastline, and there are often grand effects: towering clouds, beating waves, gleams on the rocks where Darwin, they say, once stood and pondered geological time and the ancient congress of molten stone.

But it is not these that affect me so. It is purely the light coming over the sea, a brilliant luminosity not encountered from any other vantage point in the city. It cuts me with a kind of ecstasy – as if I'm on the verge of revelation, one I'm powerless to halt. I have been brought nearly to tears, some evenings on the promenade.

There is a particular moment, when the sky goes coral pink and the breaking surf is chalk-blue, almost fluorescent in the fading light. And then each incoming swell feels as if it is rolling over my body, just under the skin, from the soles of my feet all the way to my fingernails, rolling out over the quick, making me want to reach out my fingers and touch. Although I am a controlled man, I am not immune to these things.

Controlled, that's another word I've heard people – my workmates – use to describe me. I'm a senior copywriter, moderately good at my job; good at controlling words, certainly. Words for pictures of sunsets, often with cars or couples in front of them. But I grope after language to describe the feelings I experience on my evening walks, the light in the air and on the sea. This pleases me: that some things remain beyond my grasp. That they cannot be rendered down.

Perhaps this is why I have no ambition. I've held the same position at the same agency for fifteen years and have no desire for anything greater, for a managerial position, even as the new hires are promoted around me. Such things, I know, could never fulfil my more obscure longings. I'm happy to run in place.

There are always a lot of people moving up and down the promenade: smooth-skinned models looping along in Rollerblades too heavy for their frail ankles; the old woman who sits on the same bench every evening to feed the pigeons; cheerful ladies in tracksuits, trying to shift a kilogram or two; resolute athletes with corded thighs. Dog-walkers and drug-dealers and beggars, and lovers in each other's arms as they watch the sun go down. Some of them

I have seen every other evening for the past three years, which is how long I've been taking my promenade now. Others are new. Recently, I've started to feel I recognise individual seagulls along the route, although this is surely my imagination.

One evening, a young man comes past me, sweating and steaming in a cloud of musk. Although covered up in a tracksuit, his body is obviously muscular; not the smooth, inflated-looking muscles that you see on some of the gym boys, not well-fed recreational beef, but the hard, functional build of someone who works with his body for a living. Shorter than me, but strong. He jogs fast and purposefully.

I notice him again a few days later, and from then on he intersects regularly with my evening promenade, three times a week: Mondays, Wednesdays, Saturdays. I see him going only the one way. He must loop back, as I do; but his circuit is clearly far more expansive and demanding than my own. Time-wise, he is rigid. I always pass him on my outbound trip, and always, it seems, at exactly the same place: just opposite the traffic lights where I pause to do my stretches. He waits to cross the road there, bouncing on his toes, swivelling his torso aggressively left and right. Perhaps he's heading for the gym.

Always dressed in bright, deep colours, I notice; he must have half a dozen different tracksuits, in pillar-box red, racing green, midnight blue. (These phrases come to me involuntarily.) He always wears the complete assemblage, matched top and pants, which is quite formal – never casual in a T-shirt. A white towel is looped around his neck and sometimes he grasps its ends as he waits at the traffic lights, pulling it against the back of his dark neck. A strong, almost cuboidal block of a jaw. I think he must be a boxer. Something in the way he moves, in the build. Or maybe it's just the way he holds his fists, loosely clenched, that gives me this idea.

My certainty about his occupation grows. Who but a professional athlete would need to train so often and so hard, swathed in a towel and sweat-dark tracksuit? His arms are bulkier than a long-distance runner's would need to be, he is light on his feet with a dancing stride, and there's a kind of sprightly aggression in his movements. Enormous hands, for his height. They make me self-conscious about my own flushed fists.

Two men, changeless, beating the same if opposite route; it is comforting. I've read about boxers' battles to keep their weight at certain limits, and I imagine that we are caught in the same kind of stasis. Like me, he is fighting to keep his body where it is – although, to be sure, his standard is more exacting.

After a while we start to nod to each other, cautiously. To test my boxing theory, one day I put up my fists – not sure, really, what I intend. He balls his and twitches them towards his chin. No smile, though. It feels tenuous, the moment: me with fists raised, unsure if this is a playful act.

Up close, I see the imperfections – the damaged skin of his brows, the way the scarring seems to have resulted in the loss of eyebrows. I notice that his nose looks broken, his earlobes thick. (Are those cauliflower ears?) Despite this coarsening of the features, he has an appealing face, set in an expression of youthful resolution, lit on one side by the setting sun.

It becomes a jokey ritual, a greeting every time we pass.

The lifted hands in imaginary gloves. At least, I think it's a joke. It grows from there.

One evening, when we come face to face, he and I do that little step-step dance that happens when two people are walking straight into each other: both to the same side and then both back again. I smile. His fists come up and this time he pauses to spar with me. I flinch – and then I know I'm right: only a pro could direct such a sparkling combination of quick almost-touches to my ribs, my jaw, my nose. The huge fists lunge at me, snap back; so close, I feel a tickle of warm air on my face, and smell his sweat. I raise my hands to parry.

And after that it happens every time: each evening we do the little two-step dance, and spend a few moments trading phantom blows. A smile never crosses his face, as if the scars somehow prevent it. But at the end, just before he skips to the side and jogs on, he'll give me a look and tip his chin up in brief and surely humorous acknowledgement.

A month passes, two. The woman who feeds the birds looks increasingly fragile, until I start to worry that she'll be overpowered by the sturdy pigeons bickering around her; and then one day she is gone. Shortly thereafter, I see the pigeons have constructed another old woman in their midst. The couples part and reconfigure. But the boxer and I remain the same, locked in our pattern, running and standing still.

Other people loop in other cycles around us, stitching up the ends of their days with a quick up-and-down along the water's edge. I think of ants, crawling in opposing circles; clockwise ants every now and then touching mouth-parts with their anticlockwise comrades, passing cryptic messages. Some promenaders I will doubtless never meet, caught as we are in orbits that never intersect. But the boxer and I are in sync.

My days pass mildly; I have other routines. The promenade is not my only circular occupation. I sit on Sunday afternoons in the flat and read the newspaper. I go out to buy myself coffee and croissants. I go to work, where I produce copy about faster, stronger, younger. When I hear my own words on TV, I don't remember ever writing them.

Sitting in my padded swivel chair before my computer station, hands poised to tap the keys, I am trapped in stillness. There is a strong desire to jump up and swing my arms, to dispel this immobility. But I stay where I am and the spasm passes. My colleagues at the other workstations do not notice this fleeting turmoil, do not see that I have paused in my typing to contemplate for a moment some grand gesture. I flex my hands, let them drop mildly back to the keyboard. My fingers renew their automatic labour.

Mondays, Wednesdays, Saturdays. We never speak, but our greetings are progressively more familiar. In our small, intense interactions I notice things in great detail: the fact that his irises are black, fading from that dark centre to amber rims. A chipped tooth in his slightly open mouth.

Our sparring becomes elaborate. I think he might be teaching me to box. It's all very controlled, but of course there is also a little thrill of fear. Huge fists in your face, what can you do but imagine those hands rubbing out your features, smearing your nose, forcing your teeth into your mouth? That's never happened to me of course, but I can imagine the very specific sensations: nose-break pain, tooth-shatter pain, taste of blood. I do not know exactly what the mock-blows signify – violence or camaraderie. Each thrust has the potential to explode, is centimetres from rocketing into my face, from crushing my chest. I can imagine receiving such blows far more easily than I can see myself delivering them. I try to picture pushing my hand all the way, sticking it between the big fists to press against that jaw. Impossible.

Sometimes, trotting on after our shadow-play, I am trembling slightly, feeling the sting of invisible gloves on my body, the smack of fists. I think of the phrase *glass jaw*. Compared to his stony features, I am all crystal.

One Wednesday afternoon I stay home from work with a cold. I switch on the TV at some unusual hour, to catch the afternoon news: SABC2 or 3, which I would not normally watch. And I see him, I am sure it is him, under the bright lights of the ring, in shiny red-and-white shorts, his knuckles encased in bulbous mitts like cartoon hands. His lips are distended by a gum guard, and he looks smaller with his top off, but I know him by his movements: the sideways skip and jump, fists flung out in that dancing rhythm. He and his opponent in blue are both little terrier-men – is it featherweight? – but they are pure wire-hard muscle, shiny brown with sweat. I don't catch his name over the dinging bell, the shouts of the crowd; and anyway, the commentary is in another language.

I lean forward, face close to the screen. It only lasts a couple of rounds. The one small, hard man drills the other to the floor with sweat-spraying strokes. I feel each blow as a twitch in my upper arms. And then it is over: blue lies flat on his back, toes up and out; my boxer's hands are raised above his head in victory. Blood streaming from his brow.

Only after the ads come on do I relax my hands and let myself lean backwards on the couch.

He is absent from the promenade for a week. When he reappears, I am warier of him, almost ducking away from his shadow-strokes, but he is too skilful to touch me. Often I think about speaking to him, but my mouth is dry, and he is exercising so hard, so earnestly; I don't want to break his concentration.

I am not eloquent here, in this conversation of bodies. Still, I have come to depend on these playful altercations, these little knockabouts in which neither one of us falls to the ground.

Today again, my routine is broken. What is it that delays me? A foolish thing. A flutter of wings in my chest as I'm putting on my shoes, a kind of rushing. Something to startle a man of my age. I have to sit for a few moments, gathering myself. Only fifty-four. I have had no trouble before now. I eat well; my life does not have unusual stresses. I exercise.

As a result, I am ten minutes late in getting away. Maybe twelve. I don't check the exact time of my leaving, nor do I feel the need to hurry especially, to catch up. I am rigid in my habits, but not to that degree. The heart flutter has upset me and I'm not thinking of anything else. I set out cautiously.

I do not think of the boxer, of how I have disrupted the pattern of our meetings. I do not consider that my delay will in turn mean that he is not delayed. His circuit from unknown origin to unknown destination will not, now, be paused for our customary sparring. He will not lose that five or ten seconds, and thus will cross the road five or ten seconds sooner. I do not think of these things, and if I did I would not see the significance.

I feel old and tired and a little sick; for once I do not feel like the bracing sea air, the spray, the demanding sunset light. I do not feel like meeting the radiant, youthful figure of the boxer, holding up his hands.

Ten minutes, maybe twelve. Long enough for it all to be over by the time I reach the stretch beyond the children's swings, coming up to the traffic lights. I see the small crowd ahead. A car has stopped in the road, slewed at a shocked angle, windscreen spiderwebbed. People stand with their heads down, rapt, staring at something at their centre. An ambulance pulls up. I lengthen my stride.

As I come alongside I see only people's backs. I push my way through. Cooling flesh slicked with sunscreen and sweat, joggers and walkers. A couple of dogs twisting their leashes around their owners' legs, weaving a mesh between me and what lies on the pavement. I step over crossed leashes, squeeze between shoulders.

The boxer is lying on his back, hands at his sides, legs spread, toes pointed up and away from each other. A dachshund sniffs at his bright white trainers. There is blood. My hands, the backs of my hands, tingle as if they have just been slapped. My knuckles tingle. My face aches. I back away.

I walk on. The ambulance drives past me, but it goes slowly with no siren or lights flashing. I walk and walk; something has reset my clock and I no longer know when to turn around. On beyond the café, on along the sea wall, beyond the toilets, on until the path ends at the wall of the marina and I can go no more; otherwise I might walk forever. Stepping up to the wall that blocks my path, I punch it with my left hand. Not hard, only enough to hurt my knuckles, not to bloody them; I wouldn't know how to hit that hard. I do it just once, then stand staring at the concrete for a moment before turning away.

I don't go back along the promenade. Instead I cross the road to the other side, towards the shops and hotels and away from the sea. The ocean is gentle and tired this evening. The incoming and outgoing waves seem to be confirming something, some truth about tides turning, time passing. Such flat phrases for that eternal suffering rhythm; but this is the best I can do.

I walk home a different way, through back streets. It takes me a long time. I stop halfway at a random bistro and order coffee, de-caf for the heart, and pick up the newspaper I failed to buy earlier. I don't know where I am in the day. I read the newspaper front to back, the sports pages and the classifieds and the obituaries. Then at last I continue home along an unfamiliar route. I can't avoid glimpsing, in a broken band down the steep side streets, the soft, luminous colour that the sea is generating. I can feel that brightness in the corner of my eye, but here where I am walking the world is darker. I'm cold in my T-shirt.

As I pass the window of the Woolworths on the corner, it is old, vain habit that makes me glance into the silvered glass. And I see clearly that age has come to me at last: decades, it seems, since this morning. The expensive walking clothes hang loose. And I know that from now on the years, which never burdened me before, will gather on my body, heavier and heavier in the life that remains. Time has started up again, speeding me down.

I step away from the glass and close my eyes. I raise up the boxer in my mind. Lifting my hands to my chest, I pick up the pace, one-two, one-two, elbows out. Through the evening streets, I complete my promenade.

THE LEOPARD TRAP

Daniela had taken to leaving town when things got bad. If trouble was coming – and she could usually tell – she'd take the car and go somewhere random for a few days. A nice little bed and breakfast, some place where she didn't have to explain.

In the first years of her marriage, she would never have done this: go somewhere strange, all on her own. But the trips had become necessary; she'd almost started to look forward to them. And she sensed that for Thom, too, it was some kind of relief to be out of her sight.

It had been building for the last few weeks. Thom was irritable, drinking too much, sleeping in the daytime. She knew the signs. His last bad spell had been months ago, and she'd started to relax a little. But now it was happening again. So she packed her bag and soon was heading out, before the rush-hour traffic hit.

Daniela had few commitments, apart from Thom himself. He was older, with family money as well as a partnership in an architecture firm. She'd met him when she was very young, still in college, and they'd married quickly. He'd always supported them financially. Things were simpler that way. She'd studied interior design, but she'd been out of it so long, she wouldn't know how to pick it up again, if she ever wanted to. And Thom – Thom was what she was qualified in now.

The car radio helped. Its tunes and chatter loosened the small stone of dread that lodged in her chest on days like this. She turned it on as she left Cape Town, the buildings giving way on either side to the broader contours of the countryside. The car was a new one, a convertible, and she wasn't used to it yet: her hands seemed too small on the steering wheel, as if barely holding on, her feet just reaching the pedals. She was a petite, pretty woman, with black eyes and long, silky hair. Thom could pick her up and carry her easily, like a child.

The place, near Sutherland, was a longer drive than she'd realised, and the sun had already set by the time she checked in and collected the key to her chalet. In the dark, she hardly saw the surroundings, was glad only to collapse onto the double bed, into sheets that looked like they were cast-offs from the farm family's own beds, but very clean. The places she chose for these trips were good, but not luxurious. When she checked her phone there was no reception.

She lay for a while staring up at the thatch ceiling, wondering what he was doing, whether he'd come home yet. When he was feeling this way, he sometimes stayed out drinking for hours. She worried that things might be getting worse, his dips more frequent. Perhaps they should try those pills again.

With difficulty, Daniela turned her thoughts away, directing them into a small box, one containing a few considered images. She thought about the flat. They were redoing the lounge. New paint: matte or gloss? There would be different upholstery for the lounge furniture; new cushion covers. The couch was still unworn, but it would need to be re-covered to match the look. She had to choose fabric. Sea green, she thought. With pale-gold trim.

Eventually, sleep seeped in through a crack in the lid of her quiet thoughts, and she was gone.

In the morning, Daniela emerged to find that she was very far from anything, in a flat, dry landscape. The actual farmhouse was almost invisible behind a clump of blue-gum trees. One or two other chalets perched near the main building, but hers was out on the edge, and naked without a shield of trees. Disconcerting: in the night, she had imagined herself not so distant from other sleeping people.

A faint, straight track came past from the direction of the farmhouse, with a tin arrow on a pole, pointing towards a ridge in the middle distance. The arrow said OLD LEOPARD TRAP in white-painted letters. In English not Afrikaans: for tourists.

The path was much the same texture as the bare ground on either side, and mostly distinguished by its different colour, silvery blonde against khaki. Caused, Daniela supposed, by feet scuffing the crust in a place where rain seldom disturbed it.

There was no particular reason to walk on the path rather than beside it, but she obeyed the arrow and kept to the paler strip. She was wearing thin-soled shoes – Italian leather, a gift from Thom – but perhaps it wasn't far to go.

When the path split, another signpost led her left, onto the low ridge. Coming up the rise, she nearly walked right past the trap, it was so well camouflaged; but the path stopped short and so did she. At last she divined the heap of stones to one side of the path: coffin-shaped, open at one end. It reminded her of those cases of grit that caddis-fly larvae build, but giant-sized.

It was a puzzle, set but unsolved. A trap for killing leopards, back when they still lived in these parts. Not for metamorphosis, but for ending. It looked crudely made, but it must have been skilfully put together. And strong: she could only imagine what force in a frantic cat's back and haunches might once have been thrown against its walls.

The thing drew her closer. Perhaps it was the pressure of the big sky above her – the trap was enticing, a private space. She had the curious urge to climb right in. Why not? She was half smiling as she crouched.

But it wasn't that easy. Leopards, it seemed, were smaller than she'd realised. She tucked her elbows close and wriggled on her belly into the narrow vault. It was a tight space, but long enough to fit her, head to toe.

The stones were right-angled slabs that seemed compressed from dense grey mud. The size of shoeboxes, some of them, with chinks of sky showing in between. The floor was crisp sand in which pebbles were tightly clasped, not a thing growing. Bringing her hands up awkwardly before her chin, she looked down at the dim space where the leopard's paws must have scrabbled – as if she were expecting to see prints still impressed there, a last desperate message. But nothing, just sand as smooth as if ironed. No living thing larger than an ant had touched it for years.

She saw now how the machine worked: you crawl in, exploring, perhaps lured by a bait of fatal meat; but there's no turning back. A stone is rolled across the mouth, a trapdoor drops. And then a bullet.

Shifting, she felt her shoulder rub against the rock, and her hips. She turned her head and shards of sky pressed into her eyes, blue against black. Her cheek touched stone. And all at once it struck her: the horror of the trapped creature, of the trap, this box precisely measured out for her own length and breadth ...

She whimpered and reared, bashing her head. Bright and dark patches pursued her as she struggled backwards, out and onto her feet.

And then, just as quickly, the fear was gone. Daniela looked down at the trap and it was functional again: humans at work, doing their obligatory killing. Yes, a machine to take a living cat and turn it into bones and pelt. Such things had been necessary, once. She felt her interest switch to the design of the thing. How would it work, exactly? How might she make it better, if she had sheep or goats to defend?

Now that she'd found it, it was impossible not to see the trap against its background. It was in fact quite different to the shapes of nature around it. The only related objects were the straight line of the path and the small sign on its pole at the bottom of the hill. Human things.

It was already very hot. Impatiently, she brushed the sand off her cotton blouse and trousers; she was usually so careful with her clothes. The phone, finding reception, buzzed in her pocket. Once, twice, five times. Voicemails.

They would be silent: wordless pleas from Thom, from the city. It was her voice he wanted to hear.

This would not have happened in the early days of their relationship. She would never have left his messages unreturned. She would've dropped everything and gone to his side, wherever he was. She'd tried so hard. But Daniela had learnt, since then: she knew when to shut her ears and hold her voice.

In the afternoon, showered and changed, she went over to the farmhouse, where there was a lounge and kitchen. Other visitors were there, a couple that earlier in the day she had seen striding along the path in proper hiking boots. The woman was making sandwiches: white bread with cheese. They chatted about the heat, the walk.

'We couldn't see that leopard trap,' said the woman.

'It's hard to spot,' Daniela agreed, watching the woman bear down on the bread, making squares into triangles and smaller triangles again. 'Just a big stone box. Nothing special.'

The woman appraised her, knife poised. 'You're here alone? Because, if you wanted to join us for supper ...? There's plenty.'

'Oh, that's sweet.' Daniela smiled formally. 'But I'm okay, really.'

As she left the room, the woman's smile dug into her back like a pebble. Daniela had spoken more coldly than she should have. But she knew how strangers observed her on these solitary trips: sometimes with pity, and sometimes with unseemly curiosity. Sniffing her for scandal. Often, men would try to pick her up.

One day, she thought, I might say yes. It was the first time this had occurred to her. It seemed a remote idea, one to put away for the future; but not impossible. These weekends away were such ruptures, such odd holidays from the close embrace in which she lived with Thom. She wasn't quite sure who she was, in these rented rooms, so far from the city and from home. She might do anything.

Something brought her out of sleep, into a room grown incomprehensibly dark and with no one beside her. She was afraid to raise her hands from her body or to lift her head; a breath above her face, she sensed the grit, the coldness, the weight of stones packed tight …

She sat for a moment on the edge of the bed, staring into the dark. Then she put on her thin shoes and a woollen jersey over her pyjamas and went outside.

The path was a white stain in the moonlight. She walked along it to the ridge. It was a ruthlessly clear night, pure black and silver. At the side of the trap, she knelt. In between the heaped stones there were chinks of dark. But the blackness was full and breathing, and she knew that something was in there. Just like she always knew when Thom was home, before she'd put her key in the lock.

She put her palm against the stone. It had lost every speck of sunlight it had gathered in the day, its warmth drawn down into the well of earth. She could feel the ground draining her body's warmth too. She gripped a corner block.

The stone moved unexpectedly, sliding out sideways with a hollow, grinding sound. A black breach, an exit. And a rush of relief, as if something had been held inside, like breath. She felt the wisp of a feline spirit wafting past her hands, through the broken gap in the stones and up into the roof-less night.

But after a suspended second the structure could not hold: the end of the trap collapsed with an icy clatter that Daniela felt in her chest. She stumbled backwards, tripped and crouched there for a moment.

'*Shit*,' she said aloud, but she was laughing too, exhilarated.

She breathed, calmed. Examined the damage. The moonlight now spilled inside the broken structure, where moonlight had not been for years – perhaps for centuries. Daniela bent to pick up a piece of fallen rock, about the size of a brick but much heavier. She thought for a moment of taking it home with her, a keepsake; but the idea of putting a piece of this small death-house inside her own gave her a feeling of inside-outness, and she let the slab drop to the ground.

She walked a few paces further up the ridge and tried for phone reception. Then she listened to Thom's staticky non-messages, one after the other; sounding him out, trying to discern the quality of his stillness.

She drove back to town early the next morning. The long lines of the country folded up again around the car, enclosing a landscape that grew ever closer, denser, more intricately patterned. Daniela's attention moved from the horizon and fastened itself on the dashboard, the multiplying lanes of the highway, the buildings forming up in ranks on either side. By the time she took the turn-off to home, the transformation was complete: the city rose thickly around her, stained, signed and tracked, cutting off any longer view. In one of its million niches lay Thom.

She was weary when she got to the underground parking. In the mirrored elevator, she saw that her face was sunburnt, with clownish whiteness around the eyes where her sunglasses had sat. The lift was rapid and faintly perfumed: it was an exclusive apartment block.

After opening the door to the flat, she stood completely still for a moment, to listen. Her eyes sought out the damage. In the past, she had come back to find dislocated plumbing, doors pulled off hinges, pictures from frames. Thom directed his despair always against material things. It was not a chaotic violence, but rather a grimly driven dismantling. This time, the backrest of the sofa had been laid open, the stuffing protruding from a slit like something that had long desired release. Beneath the expensive upholstery were folded wads of yellow foam, cheap pine boards tacked together. In one place the skirting board had been levered away from the wall, revealing a black gap that went down who knew how far – perhaps beyond the concrete and pilings of the building and into the cold earth itself.

The air was rank. He would have stayed inside, not eating or bathing, with the windows closed. She moved around the flat, opening up, letting out the sour smell. Again she felt the passing of black spirits over her hands. With every bolt undone, there was release; some pressure was relieved.

She tidied a little, righting chairs and closing cupboard doors. Some dents in the wooden floorboards; a pile of broken glass from a lampshade. A brief rage passed through her like a flush of blood, and was as quickly gone: at his frailty, his lack of will. Why could he not, just once, go further; do damage that could not be so easily undone? Rip the skin right off.

But no. She would mend and smooth, as before. And they would continue. Truly, she felt distant from the physical damage. It had always been Thom's flat, not hers. Designed by him, paid for by him. Daniela thought instead, and for the first time, about the people who'd built these rooms, and who would now be paid to repair them. She had seen blueprints, of course, but had never before been curious about the process of building, of raising the plans off the page. Someone must've laid bricks, one by one; someone must've covered them with these smooth coats, these tiles and plaster and paint.

She circled slowly, wiping, fixing, setting to rights. Her circle turned closer and closer around the bedroom, the bed, the man, until she could no longer avoid him, and she knelt by his side at the edge of the mattress, hands resting on her thighs. She felt calm now; tender. She could smell the spent arousal coming off his flesh.

Thom was lying quietly, fully clothed under the covers. She knew the exhaustion that overtook him, afterwards. He would not remember everything. He would wake soon and have to piece it together from the evidence.

He opened red eyes.

Thom, she said.

He blinked at her.

She put out a hand and pressed a strand of damp hair back behind his ear. Thom, she said again.

Behind her she could hear the sounds of the day coming in through opened windows. She sensed, too, a door that might be opened, that she might pass through if she chose. Thom turned his head so that her hand lay over his dry lips. He opened his mouth slightly around her fingers and she felt the heat within. Thom, she thought. Thom.

And even in that moment, her hand touching his face, she could not tell exactly what she was: leopard or hunter. The one inside the box of stones, or the one who stands and watches as the trap falls closed, over and over again.

LIMERENCE

It took only three days to find him, this time. Turned out he was very close, just across the road from her house and up in the air, painting a white wall blue. When she saw him, her heart did all the things a heart must do: it swelled, it leapt, it skipped a beat. She crossed without looking left or right and stopped directly under the ladder – because, of course, it had already happened to them both. The terrible luck.

She gripped a rung and looked up between his legs. A drop of paint spun from his roller to land on her cheek. She didn't flinch. From this angle, his throat and upturned chin seemed not quite human, the soft underjaw of a frog or a fish. She shook the ladder lightly, made him look.

for we are two stars falling in the night sky

It wasn't that he was her type, particularly. No one was her type, until all at once they were. Rough or smooth, hard or soft, dark or light – what did it matter? Certainly, he was the loveliest man in the world (again, again and always). Such fingernails, such knees and ears, and that taut crescent of belly visible under the hang of his paint-flecked T-shirt. Whatever type he was, it was the one, the only, every time; the only one for her was here, was him.

She said hello.

The man came down the ladder in a clatter of boots and knuckles. 'Alright, love?'

'I'm crazy about you,' she said. 'I've been thinking about you for days.' When she touched his face, he flinched. 'Sorry,' she said. 'Sorry about this.'

They kissed: a sweet preliminary, not deep. This was the best part, the last pure moment. For these few lush beats, the fever stilled.

His skin against her palm was cool, like something vital had already left.

beloved
        before thy beauty kingdoms tremble

Three days earlier, she'd woken up sick. Ah crap, she thought, not now. But it was undeniable. She could feel the condition rising to the surface, scuttling up the nerve fibres, claw over claw. It announced itself in all the usual ways: the night before she'd been restless, weepy; this morning there was an ache in her womb and her breasts were tender. Painfully sharp senses bullied her out of bed, eyes watering in the sun-flare, the pillow rough against her cheek. Her body felt icy – t-shirt soaked with sweat – but her face was fever-hot. She could smell the grass from outside, and the neighbour's coffee.

Oh, and the sounds. Someone was playing music in the flat upstairs, a love song of course, Oh baby, and there she was, tearing up like a moron.

Fuck.

When she called in sick, her boss at the PR company was sympathetic. She was a model employee – unruffled, dependable – despite these occasional bouts of illness. 'My girl, you need to start looking after yourself,' he told her. 'We're none of us as young as were.'

The symptoms advanced predictably. Her head grew light and her heart weighty, waterlogged; but it also seemed too strong, wanting to jump from her chest. Nausea, as rich compounds rinsed through her blood. Grimly, she noted she was low on supplies. Vitamins. Paracetamol. Condoms.

The first spasm hit while she was waiting in line at the chemist. A wrench in the groin, *fuck*. The man in the queue in front of her half-turned and gave her a look of quickened but impersonal interest: some pheromonal tendril tickling his back-brain. She managed to return a cool glance.

She felt malnourished, missing an essential mineral. The smell of the sweets at the till filled her mouth with saliva, but the thought of eating was sickening. Her reflection in a mirrored pillar was a vision of hunger. Lips full and parted, mouth a ripe fruit split to show its seeds.

There was an ad for blood-pressure meds on the wall, with a middle-aged couple in each other's arms; she had to look away. And Christ, the music. It was everywhere, piped through the walls. Songs of yearning. Songs of losing and finding. She tried not to listen, but the lyrics kept tripping her up: blunt lurches of the heart.

This part might go on for a week – two weeks, if she was

unlucky. She went to bed early each night, but slept no more than a couple of hours. She cried in the dark. Solid food was repulsive, but she drank lots of water and took her vitamins. It was important to conserve energy, but also stupid to delay. Best to go all out from the start, while you still have strength. By day ten she'd be ravening. Weeping in public at the first dumb notes of the chorus.

Her heart was going at a constant eighty-five beats a minute. She counted.

She hadn't bothered with doctors for years, but there'd been a time, in the beginning, when she'd tried to get help. Age twenty-one, she'd waited on a hard bench at the women's health clinic, hands clasped in her lap, between a pregnant lady and a teenager wanting the pill.

What was strange was that her right thumb could feel her left, but not vice versa – the left was rubbery, like something from a joke shop. She stroked it lightly. She was remembering holding hands with her first boyfriend, in high school. Before all this. They'd kissed, and he'd touched her breasts. Perhaps they'd gone further, or it was unclear how far they'd gone. She couldn't quite recall.

A nurse was calling her name.

The doctor, an overworked gynaecologist, seemed somewhat out of her depth. 'So, these episodes, these ... encounters. They cause you distress?'

'Look, not all the time. Like now, I'm totally fine. Super calm. Not feeling much of anything.'

'I see. Perhaps you're a bit depressed?'

'Not really.'

'Or something else is bothering you.'

'Well.' She held out her left thumb. 'I am *literally* not feeling, here. It's been sort of numb for a few weeks now. Since the last time.'

The doctor took her hand. 'Can you feel this?'

There was pressure, but it was distant, as if through a glove. 'Mm.'

She closed her eyes while the doctor squeezed other bits and pieces: arms, toes, shoulders. Funny, she couldn't think of his face, that first boyfriend. What she recalled was the sweetness and simplicity of their exchange. Pleasure for pleasure, touch for touch. Was this how it was for other people, all the time?

The doctor was saying something, but her voice was far away.

'Sorry, what?'

'I said, are you still with us? You were drifting off there.' The doctor was writing a worried note. 'I'm sending you to a specialist.'

She came away with a handful of pamphlets: guidance for healthy eating, for handling stress, for safer sex.

my sweet lover comes to me on the perfumed wind

The search. The important thing was to position yourself to survey large numbers of men. It meant a lot of walking around: days and nights pounding the pavement, eyes peeled. She used to go out to the clubs, but with age and experience she'd bothered less with setting. It could happen anywhere, she knew now, any time. Some enchanted evening, sure – but also eight o'clock in the morning in the parking lot behind Liquor City. You had to be prepared.

She carried condoms, although often she forgot about them in the moment. It made no real difference – things didn't work that way – but she did fear pregnancy. It hadn't happened yet, and perhaps it never could. What space for a child in this body, after all?

Fortunately, the condition gave you stamina, a fevered drive to keep scanning, face after face, body after body. So many variations on the basic phrasing: eyes and mouths, strides and postures. Could you be? Could you be loved? All could, potentially. Surely almost all had been desired, if only once in their lives. But not by her, not today. She was looking for the man she'd been dreaming of, weeping for; his face had not yet been revealed, but soon, soon she would see him in full. And then – then he'd be dreaming too.

She went home, threw up bile, drank a bottle of wine with some painkillers, checked herself in the bathroom mirror. She looked fantastic: flush-cheeked, black-eyed. A woman in the throes.

The specialist was young and eager in his white coat, keen to take her blood. He had an image already pulled up on his computer when she walked through the door. 'Bingo,' he said, swivelling the screen for her to see. The scene was pretty. A scattering of pale-gold globules, like drops of oil, drifting through a school of rosy doughnuts.

''The yellowish structures, in between the corpuscles? Those are your bad guys, right there.'

'Wait. This is blood? These things are in my blood?'

He explained: in the dormant phase of the disease, a small concentration of the organism remained, slopping in the bilges of the body. But in a flare-up, it would rouse, multiply, invade – blood, lymph, saliva, mucus membranes, sexual fluids. This triggered the production of neurotransmitters, the ones involved in arousal and attachment. 'Oxytocin, dopamine, vasopressin, the usual culprits. Basically, you're primed. As you've noted, this results in certain, uh, behavioural changes in the host.'

The gracious hostess, she thought. He told her the name: a word she didn't know, Latin maybe. 'I've never heard of it.'

'It's pretty rare. And people with the diagnosis – well, they generally prefer to keep it quiet.'

An ancient parasite squeamishness was crawling up her back. Those golden grains clustering, latching on like ticks. Prickles of revulsion and fascination ran through her body, toes to scalp, from her belly to the tip of every hair-fine nerve. 'So I can take something for it, then. To get rid of it.'

'Ah, oh,' the doctor said. 'No.'

'Antibiotics?'

'I'm afraid not. It's a virus.'

She stared at him. There was an odd itchiness around her heart, unscratchably deep. A tickle at her wrists. Minute creatures ferreting in her veins.

'You're telling me there's no treatment? At all?'

'Well. Our priority is obviously containment. Preventing transmission. During the active phase, some people find tranquilisers helpful? One of my patients – hah! – checks in to a secure clinic for the duration.' He seemed nervous, as if she might jump on him without warning. 'Unfortunately, there's not much we can do about the cumulative damage.'

'You mean the numbness.'

'Also flattened affect. Emotional muting. You may have noticed.'

'I guess.'

It was true. Beyond the visceral shudder, there was no real fear. Stick her with a pin, she wouldn't flinch, or be much surprised, either.

Things could be worse, the doctor told her. There were more destructive strains of the disease. Some unfortunates were in the florid state almost constantly; their stressed and hypersensitised bodies tended to burn out young. 'But mental attitude is so important,' he concluded. 'This is a manageable condition. The vast majority of my patients go on to lead long and rewarding lives.'

On his monitor, the animalcules continued on their way, sculling through calm plasma seas.

> *his terrible arrows pierce me*
> *and sickness seizes my heart*

Now that she knew what it was, things started to make sense. She understood her history with the condition. Its genesis.

It had come to find her at nineteen: an undergrad, sweaty after a campus hockey match. There was this man, a grey-haired guy in a cardigan, like someone's granddad, who'd been watching from the sidelines the whole way through the game. As she bent to drink from the tap by the changerooms, he came striding down the field, closing the distance too rapidly, before she could react. He was a big man, with a broad face that might have been kindly if not so rigid and flushed with need. He gripped her shoulders and stared into her eyes, as if about to give her some diffi-cult message, full of wonderment and urgency. She didn't pull away. Something was waking up, deep in her body. Curiosity: cellular, naive. A stranger at the gates.

She'd never kissed anyone old. His teeth felt brittle against her tongue. Her mouth tingled with pinpricks of recognition, of atavistic warning. She let him take her hand, let him lead her away.

'Sorry for that,' he said when they were done.

She got shakily out of his car, still holding her hockey stick. 'No, no it's alright,' she said, and laughed. 'It's quite alright.'

And what was that, what fucked-up shit was THAT, she was thinking as she walked away. Nothing it was nothing don't think about it. She was laughing again, she couldn't stop. It was exhilarating, as if she'd lain down in the path of an avalanche and stood up again unscathed. (But no, that's not how it goes; you lie down for an avalanche and then you die, you're already dead ...) When she got home she fell across her mattress in her hockey kit and slept for fourteen hours.

And afterwards, so sick. In bed for weeks, uncomprehending. First cut is the deepest, like they say. It took her a long time to work out what to do, what she needed. A few false turns before she got it right.

'Every time,' she said, 'I lose a little more.'

This was doctor number three, some years later. He was an elderly man with an impassive manner. He listened to her speak. He did not interject. She touched her ribs on the left side. 'It's this bit now.'

It wasn't that sensation disappeared altogether. It returned in force when she was sick, of course; and then retreated further, as if each attack blew a few more fuses.

The numb patches were cloud shadows on her skin, slipping from hands to lips to thighs. 'But that's not what upsets me. It's this.' She moved her hand to her chest, over her heart. Cheesy, but that did seem to be where the absence was located. 'I don't feel ... it's like I don't have the capacity ...'

'Loss,' he said. 'Progressive loss. Of joy, of pain. Farewell to desire. This is what we can expect.'

She let the hand fall.

He watched her for a moment. 'Some people find it helpful to expose themselves to stimuli,' he said, not unkindly. 'Visual materials.'

'What, porn?' She laughed. Embarrassment was one of the first emotions to go, necessarily. 'Doesn't do much for me, these days.'

'Then something else. To stir the heart. Music?'

Before this all began, she'd liked music well enough. Had gone out dancing, like any young person. She shook her head. Music was the worst.

'Then poetry.' He took a small green book from a shelf. It was cloth-bound and battered, like something from a junk-shop bargain bin. She took it gingerly. *Erotic Verse from the Ancient World*. In general, she preferred not to read about other people's loves.

'Take it,' said the doctor. 'I myself have found some comfort in its pages.'

It sat on her desk for a week, like homework. She was reluctant to touch it. But eventually she braced herself and opened the table of contents. Greeks in love, Sumerians in love, Abyssinians, Mughals, Mayans. She turned the pages.

for love is pomegranate wine
is cool antimony

oh my bridegroom I tremble before thee
in the bedchamber I would caress thee
my lion my bridegroom

on this dark earth the fairest thing

She pushed the book away. All those old poets, lovestruck, lovesick; sick to death, every last one of them. It made her angry.

Still, she kept *Erotic Verse* for a while. She found herself opening it, every now and then: quick peeks, just long enough to catch a phrase, a couplet, sweet and sore. Long after she'd had to return the book to the doctor, lines repeated on her, coming back up like heartburn. Especially when something was brewing. When the illness was almost upon her again.

The condition grants some mercies, some powers. Dilated pupils, flushed cheeks, taut breasts: they never could say no, the men. She grasped the front of his T-shirt and pulled him away from the ladder, into the carport next door and down onto the concrete floor. She got his work-pants around his knees, high on the scents of his armpits and groin and his turpentine hands. Loving it, loving it all, his hardening cock, his navel, the stray dark hairs on his shoulders and the freckles on his thighs; the fissures under his nails the funnels of his ears the cave of his mouth, the crevices the follicles the pores the points of entry. Her love grown sharp, needling under the skin. She straddled him, pushed him down when he tried to turn.

> *one thousand kisses*
>
> > *give me*

'What?' he gasped, pulling away for a moment. 'What did you say?'

She pressed her mouth to his, tongued him wider and would not let him pull away. He was inside her now but by this point that was not the point, was beside the point, the point had shifted; had forced itself up from her groin and into her chest and her throat, insisting, needing to be delivered by the mouth. She worked her tongue deep, making sure that every glowing syllable was stowed.

> *ten thousand*
>
> > *kisses   more   and more*

A million barbed seeds, a river of them, coursing through her body into his, binding them lips to lips and loins to loins; lacerating, tearing at membranes strained and inflamed, dragging her insides out – and just as the pain became too much to bear, a bone-twanging jerk in her pelvis as something convulsed, ripped free and coughed up out of her and   *oh*

> *and oh   it shakes my heart*
>
> > *it shakes the heart in my bosom*

She drew back, and watched him shudder and groan and swallow it down. A moment's stillness and then his shoulders stiffened and his neck flung back; his skull whacked the concrete and his eyes rolled up.

She eased herself off him, panting. Too dizzy to stand. Her skull was a blown eggshell; her torso the chrysalis of something violently hatched and flown.

> *hence my tears fall like rain*
> *hence my sorrows are abundant*

The man lay quietly, drained, filled. Gently, she pushed his slack jaw closed. He was OK-looking. Full lips, deep black hair. A stocky, strong body. A cold sore on the corner of his mouth, skin scarred with old acne. As always, she wished briefly that things had gone a little slower. That there'd been time to lie beside him, to learn his real face, perhaps to speak, even. To do these tender things.

But that was silly. Already her body was reconfiguring. Muscles relaxing, skin cooling. Objects losing their haloes. She picked the fleck of paint from her cheek and spat out the sour taste in her mouth.

His eyes flickered open. 'Wait,' he said. 'Wait, what?'

'Sorry,' she said. Her voice was hoarse, as if she'd been shouting. Maybe she had.

She could see he was starting to hear the music already, some knowing, tender tune starting up in his head. 'What?' he repeated, fearful.

She should say more. Wish him luck, maybe, offer some tips. But her throat was sore and she was extremely tired. And oh, just look at the state of her, on her knees on the ground. As she got to her feet, he reached out to trail his fingers down her ankle, but she stepped away smartly. Pulled her skirt straight. Slight revulsion.

On the way home she stopped at a fast-food joint and ordered a toasted-cheese sandwich. Hunger, thirst: those mild and undisturbing appetites. She set her tray down at a table near the back. There was a young couple sitting in the booth opposite, leaning into each other, shoulders and thighs touching casually as they ate. It was a peaceful time, these few hours afterwards. Her heart felt small and buoyant, its light beat barely perceptible. She examined her pale hands. Blood ebbing, pulling back from her extremities. She wondered how much further there was to go; how much still to lose.

Poor guy. It was all just beginning, for him. Tomorrow he'd wake up feeling so shit. Dread, fever, yearning. The palpitations, the bubbles of adrenalin, the painful arousal. Or whatever stuff went on with men – who really knew? It was good that he'd seemed sturdy. She always felt bad about the frail ones.

Most times, the specialist had told her, the disease was unidirectional. But in rare recorded cases, a sufferer turned around and fed the virus back to its prior host, then received it again in a toxic feedback loop. Two people might stay together like that for years, ecstatically reinfecting in complex cycles of dormancy and flare-up, until the strain became too great. At the time, she'd felt wistful to hear this. Her disease was the ordinary, lonely kind, passing itself ever forward, never repaid.

She bit into the sandwich. It was bland and filling.

Already, spots of numbness were settling on her tongue, her little toes, the tip of her nose.

The lovers were whispering to each other. She could hear nothing, not even her own jaws chewing. No sound without, no sound within. But she supposed there must be music playing, in a place like this. There usually was.

THE BOULDER

When the boulder came down from the mountainside, it must've made a sound like the end of the world, rocking the ground with each thunderous landing and recoil. It must've sung through the air, thrashing the bush on the slope into a sappy pulp with every bounce, on its way to embed itself in the lawn of the luxury holiday home below.

Dan did not hear or see this passage. He slept deeply, as teenagers do, waking only when the last impact shuddered the foundations of the house. He knew immediately what it was, though. Not an earthquake, not a bomb. His first thought on waking was this: *the mountain is falling on top of us.*

In the ensuing silence, he didn't even sit up. It was not his house, after all, not his place to investigate. The two collie dogs that had slept in the room with him both went to sit at the closed door, as if expecting a visitor, but they didn't bark. No other footsteps in the house. Dan lay very very still, playing dead, until the trick seemed to work and he slipped back under, into sleep.

It was late morning when he woke again. He dressed and walked through the silent house, opened the glass sliding door into the back garden and saw what had happened. Half the lawn had been replaced by a grey-brown boulder as high as the house. The rock was two-tone, raw side up, stained brown where the earth had held it. It looked like something from another planet, bearing traces of a different world. A few crushed fronds were trapped in its crevices, trailing the sharp, sweet smell of high mountain places.

The more nervous dog – Jessie – trembled at his heels, while Jax snuffled around the base of the boulder. Dan was trembling too. The rock seemed precarious: the lawn, at a slight rake, was on the verge of tipping it towards him. The slightest touch might send the monster sliding again, right over him and through the glass doors and on into the house.

But after he'd stared at the monumental guest for a while longer, it seemed clear that the boulder had chosen its place of rest. It didn't creak or shift. He went a little closer.

The rock had not had an easy descent – it was bruised, with paler stone showing through on the scuffed edges. One small impact mark, at eye level, was almost perfectly circular, a neat scoop of strawberry pink. He thought of Colette: a touch of delicacy on the scarred brow of the stone.

He reached out, then pulled his hand away. The scene should not be disturbed. Because had there not been a crime here somehow? Damage? Looking up, he could see the boulder's destructive spoor, a clear trail all the way up to a patch of exposed soil on the ridge. Surely someone would want to know who was responsible? And here, the evidence looming over him, undeniable.

Dan went back inside. He took the dirty wine glasses into the kitchen and put them in the sink. He picked up Colette's shoes and carried them to the main bedroom.

The bed was empty.

He was sixteen and Colette, a year and a half older, was his very first girlfriend. She was a slender girl with light, curling hair. At times her long, fine-boned face, with its delicately flaring nostrils, made him think of an ivory horse in a chess set. They'd known each other for only a few months. Now it was summer, and she'd invited him to spend a week of the holidays in her family beach house.

'I'll meet your folks?' he asked, nervous.

'No, are you crazy?'

So it would just be the two of them. He hid his amazement.

'I go there all the time,' she said. 'My parents are cool with it.'

Dan was husky, large for his age. He was reminded that Colette had not yet guessed how young he really was.

The holiday was the most exciting thing that had ever happened to him. Colette came to pick him up in a shiny little car, the dogs bundled in the back with her bags. He felt bad not to be the one driving – too young for a license – and steeled himself to do it anyway if she asked him to take the wheel; but she didn't. In the end it didn't matter: he felt so buoyed just to be there, heading out to the coast in a car with a girl like this, into the shimmering blue, that it felt like he was propelling the car with the force of exhilaration alone.

But once they got to the house – which was huge, white,

and filled with light and views of aqua water – he became awkward, unsure of what they were there to do. His parents were small-town people, inland folks. They'd never had holiday houses, or holidays really, and he didn't know quite how to behave. The ocean watched through the tall plate-glass windows, waiting for his move.

In the first few days he and Colette had sex several times – which was still astonishing to him, barely believable. Otherwise, all she wanted to do was suntan, in the garden or on the beach, five minutes away on the other side of the road. He went with her, but secretly he felt a yearning in the other direction: up, to the topmost point of the high rocky ground that lay behind the houses.

The big windows and patio doors woke tingles in his scalp. Once, when he was ten, on a school trip to the public swimming pool, he'd run in his bathing trunks towards the glitter of water and instead slammed head first into the shock of a glass wall. He remembered the dumb halt of it, and then a blank. Waking up a few moments later, he'd felt at first a nameless despair, and later shame. It still gave him a quake of strangeness, to think of that missing moment, black as space. Thick head, he remembered the teacher saying. That's what saved you.

'Great view,' he said to Colette. It was not the first time he'd made this observation.

'Mm,' she said. 'I told them to get burglar bars, but Mom and Dad love having it open like this. All the light. Anyway, we've got the alarm, and serious security. Those guys are here in like two minutes, with guns. Plus they cruise past every half hour.'

'Great,' he said. 'I'll try not to look too suspicious.'

She gave him a laugh, a full, genuine one, and he laughed back in relief. He said to himself: maybe she is waiting for you to be decisive, to show her something new. That is what a boyfriend does.

You could just say: *I want to go up the mountain today.* Or, better:

Let's go up the mountain.

So that's what he did say. Just like that.

'Ah ...' she said. 'Let's not, and say we did.' She was reading the label on a bottle of suntan oil. Already she had on her tangerine-coloured bikini.

He flushed. 'Sure, no, I just thought ...'

'You can go, if you want,' she said, smoothing the oil onto her legs. 'Go. Take the dogs, they're driving me nuts.'

There was no path. Dan climbed up as high as he could, Jessie and Jax running ahead, until he could see over the crest of the hill and almost into the valley beyond. Near the top, the boulders were heaped up against the side of the mountain, waiting their turn like huge, slow children on a diving board. You could see where others had already rolled and come to rest on the slope below. Right down at the bottom, some had been built into the fabric of the houses, the road, the sea wall. The dogs came back to see what had made him stop, fussing at his legs. 'Okay, okay, I'm here,' he said, slapping their flanks. Dan had almost come to think of them as his own: a team, hunter and his pack. He laughed at himself – and the idea of Colette in an apron, waiting for him to bring something for the pot. And with these silly hounds, not even hunting dogs, sheepdogs who'd never seen a sheep. He clicked his tongue at them, and together they continued along the ridge.

There was dampness on his upper lip and under his arms. Around him the mountain sweated and shifted too. When he came down he would be smelling, scratched up; did he want her to see him like that? He wasn't sure. Maybe she liked that sort of thing; maybe it was his roughness that she wanted. Anyone's guess. But odour, that rankness under his arms – no girl would be into that, surely.

One last boulder blocked his way to the summit. He kicked at its base. There was no danger of shifting it: the rock was deeply rooted. It was like kicking at the earth's core. Nonetheless, he thought, with the next rains things would tumble, rearrange. Mountains were always falling down.

He laid his cheek against it, smelling the cool greenish-grey of the stone. Then he gripped and started to climb, finding the holds and ridges by touch, clumsy but strong. Granite was harder to climb than sandstone – not so many cracks. It hurt his fingers. Halfway up, he imagined Colette watching him from below and it almost made him slip.

Since they'd arrived here, he'd been holding himself so stiff next to her, terrified of breaking something. Trying to tell when it was okay to touch her and when not. Now it was good to move. To sweat, and not worry about sweating.

At the top, he stood and looked down. The waves were coming in neatly in thin white rolls. Turquoise lozenges of swimming pools gleamed. Land and sea took on their proper proportions, seen from this height: the world was ocean. Such a sombre blue. It made the colour of the pools seem frivolous.

From above, the shapes of the big houses were eccentric, with whorls and curlicues, like multi-chambered seashells.

Each one three times the size of his own home, but oddly flimsy: the fallen boulders looked so much more solid.

Colette's parents owned one of the larger houses, well placed for sea views. He found the broad driveway, the double garage, the patch of grass at the back and the small pink rectangles of the deckchairs.

There was a pale fleck moving diagonally across the green of the lawn. He deciphered it: Colette, settling herself in a deckchair. She'd be lying there all day, in her giant sunglasses.

It was strange to see her so reduced. Although she was not a large person, usually she loomed over him, close up, filling his vision. Strange also to realise that, for the moment, he was glad not to have his face pressed up against that flesh – glad just to breathe. He hated the smell of suntan oil.

Breath had sometimes been hard for him, these last few days, with Colette growing ever more beautiful in the sun. In the evenings, they sat down to eat at the long table in the dining room. She liked to dress for dinner: lipstick, hair up, shoes with a heel. It made her look older, even, than she'd seemed to him before. Usually, she ordered in – but not pizza: exotic restaurant food, always several different dishes. She did not seem to expect him to pay, for which he was silently thankful. They ate from porcelain plates with silver cutlery, and drank fine wine from the extensive rack.

He knew they should be making conversation, like a man and a woman on a date, but he sat searching for words. The formal dining arrangement made it worse. Each night he said less and drank more. There were periods of silence, with Colette staring out of the window at the darkening sea, or checking her cellphone for messages. The dogs kept watch from the corner of the room.

On the sideboard stood family photos in heavy silver frames. Mother, father, Colette as a baby, an older brother. The whole family had a similar look: lean, with attractive, slightly elongated features and pale eyes.

Dan's eyes were the colour of the dark slate floors in the second bathroom. This thought had occurred to him the night before, when he'd escaped the awkwardness at the table to go to the bathroom. He'd sat on the toilet, guts uneasy, examining the marks in the tile. Knowing that Colette was waiting in the room next door, ablaze, expectant.

Up on the rock, Dan felt a dreamy vertigo. Like he might topple onto her, all the way down there. He imagined something happening to her at that moment: an assault, a seizure, a horrible accident. He would see it all reduced, the kicks and struggles – tiny flickers against the green grass. Maybe, a fraction of a moment later, a thin cry floating up through the air. He'd be too far away to prevent it, to catch or hold her – to be held accountable. He was much too high.

So high, there was nothing but blue sky all around him, no substance, nothing to lean on. He swayed. A tremor shook his legs and he went down on his knees, clutching the rock.

He was able to crawl away from the edge. The other side of the rock turned out to be easier, sloping gently. At its base he crouched in the bushes, legs still shuddering. The dogs licked his face. All he'd wanted was to be up there, at the top.

At dinner, miraculously, despite his clumsiness and the constant slight trembling that he was feeling now in Colette's presence, he didn't break a thing, or bite a section out of the rim of his glittering wine glass. He drank glass after glass, and the more he drank the brighter and more finely drawn her face seemed on the other side of the polished table top. Her eyes so bright he could not look.

She was going to dump him. He knew it absolutely. He looked at the cream and silver surfaces of the house, and felt his wrongness there quite clearly. The house could not tolerate his touch. He didn't know how to stand here, how to sit or hold things. Of course this was plain to her as well, and any minute now she would dump him. He was quite drunk.

When her phone rang, she stared at the screen for a moment without answering.

'Who is it?' he asked, too loudly.

Instead of replying, she took the phone through into the bedroom to talk.

'Who was it?' he said when she came back.

'What? Dan, god,' she said, dropping into her seat. She kicked off her grown-up shoes and pulled her feet up into the chair.

'Who?'

'It was my dad, okay? Look, I'm sorry, but he wants to come out here tomorrow.' She didn't look at him. 'And anyway I think it's better, don't you?'

'What? What do you mean? What's better?'

She sighed. 'Dan ...' She would leave him, she would dump him, she was doing it now: he could see her mouth shaping the words. But he couldn't hear her, only his own voice, noisy in his head. 'Was that really your dad?' he said. 'You don't have to lie. If you want me to go, just say it.'

She spread her fingers on the table, examined their tips. 'Yeah. I'm saying it.'

That night, he ended up in the spare bedroom with the dogs. And by morning the boulder was there.

The sun was already high, and the boulder had almost no shadow, just a thin rim of black around its base. Now Dan recognised the rock – it was the one he'd met before, up on the slope. Here was that particular lip that he'd used as a grip, just canted over. He could climb it easily now.

Jax and Jessie hung back, tails waving uncertainly. Dan squatted down and peered into the crevice under the rock. His thumbs tingled, recalling being hit by hammers, caught in car doors. He lay on his stomach and put his face as close as he could, but saw nothing in the darkness. When he put his hand flat against the ground and slid it in, his fingertips touched something rough and dry. He worked it back and forth until he could pull it free and into the light – and fell back on his arse, staring at the thing in his hand. A splintered wooden slat, still attached to a strip of deck-chair canvas, candy pink. *Fuck*. He hurled the thing into the flowerbed, yelling '*No!*' to Jax as the anxious dog went after it.

He hurried into the house. Black spots mottled his vision. The living room was dim, but he did not switch on a light. Out the front, her car was still in the driveway. He sat for a while on the huge white couch, heart hitting the front of his chest. He took out his phone to call her, but then put it away without dialling. When he tried a second time a minute later, it went straight to voicemail. Swallowing back the sickness, he went outside to peer again at the boulder, underneath it, careful not to touch it with any part of his body. He'd kicked at that thing, up there on the mountain, only yesterday. The dogs trailed him back and forth, hoping for reassurance.

He sat again on the couch, big as a bed. The sweat cooled in his palms, and he wiped them on the white fabric. What to do? Phone someone? The police ...? Her *dad*? Each thought produced a hard thrust of panic in his throat, like something was trying to ram its way out. To keep it down, he took huge gulps of air and held them, counting, as he waited for them all to come and find him there.

All at once there were cars drawing up outside, a clatter at the door, a strange man's voice. Without thinking, he was up from the couch, through the glass doors and out into the garden, not looking back.

He squeezed in behind the boulder. It was the first time he'd actually touched it since its fall. Here the neat boundary of the garden had been breached: he saw uprooted tree stumps, split stems, mashed petals. The garden wall had been smashed through, but it would be impossible to climb out over the big shards of precast concrete; anyway, directly behind the property an overgrown bank rose steeply, impassable. There was no way out.

Only a strip of lawn was visible from where he stood. There was a moment of quiet, in which he breathed in the smells of dog shit and damp soil, and then he heard the patio door slide open.

The man's voice again, deep, and shadows moving on the lawn. Shadow people merging, separating. Shadow dogs. A man came into sight, pacing backwards across the grass. Lean build, pink polo shirt, thinning sandy hair. He stopped dead and gazed up at the boulder, hand slapped against his forehead in what might be amazement or horror. 'Colette!' he shouted.

Silence. The man remained frozen, staring.

'Bloody hell,' he said more quietly.

Dan recognised him now, from the pictures in the silver frames.

Her father.

'Bloody hell!' he said again. 'Colette!'

And then he was shaking his head and – could it be? – laughing, and gesturing towards the house. A slim figure sidled into the crook of his arm. Arms folded, coy and fidgeting, digging a toe into the grass like a kid. Dan let out the breath he felt he'd been holding all morning.

'We should get that chappie from the *Cape Times* in here,' the father continued. 'Photographer chappie. They'll want this for the front page. Can you climb up there, Col? Get one of you on top – in your bikini. Hey?'

'Dad,' she said, rolling her eyes.

She swivelled out of his clasp, arms still clutched across her chest.

Dan could see she was tense – shooting glances back at the house.

It's me, he thought. I'm not supposed to be here.

And for the first time in all the time he'd been with her, he knew what she was thinking.

He liked the dogs. They were gentle with him and well trained, never barking, just giving their alert attention where it was needed. Which is what they did now, coming to sit directly in front of him, side by side, pointing their snouts at him with quiet, friendly curiosity.

But the father was already going back into the house. 'I need a drink, sweetheart,' Dan heard him rumbling.

Colette remained standing on the lawn, hip cocked, arms crossed, swaying a little left and right as if in a light breeze. As she rocked he saw her eyes take in the dogs, pause, adjust, then follow their gaze to find him there. Her small personal breeze stilled completely.

Only hours before, he would've been mortified, would've shrunk away from those eyes, would've wriggled more deeply into the crack or rolled over onto his back like one of the dogs. But now he just stood there.

She gave him a small smile, and for a single moment there was something between them that had never been there before: some kind of recognition. He saw a glimpse of what that might be like, for two people to look at each other frankly, without fear. Perhaps it was possible to show himself to her again, differently. To start over.

He was stepping out from the shade of the boulder, feeling a hesitant gladness, when she glanced at the house and her smile stopped short. Without moving her body she gave a tense shake of the head. No. One finger lifted from her forearm, stilling him. Another look at the house, and then she stepped closer.

'Where did you go?' he asked.

'Out for breakfast,' she said in a low voice. 'But I couldn't keep him away all morning.' She folded her arms tighter. 'Dan, what are you doing here?'

He still had one hand against the cool of the stone.

'You were supposed to be gone already. I told you. I *told* you. Last night.' She looked at the rock with disgust. 'And this –'

'Colette,' came a call from the house.

She glanced over her shoulder. 'Just ... I don't know. Just don't let him see you. We'll sort it out later, okay?'

She turned her back on him and walked away.

He was still standing like that, one foot forward, pointing like one of the dogs, when he heard the front door open and close – and then the four beeps of the alarm setting itself.

It took him a moment to realise what had happened. He came out from behind the rock and stood on the grass. There was no movement inside. He cupped his hands and peered through the patio door, tried the handle. It wouldn't move.

'Colette?'

He rattled the door. Banged his fist against the glass. She'd never given him a set of keys.

'Colette!'

Now the dogs were whimpering by his side, scrabbling at the doorframe. They were not used to this treatment either. Dan backed away blindly, came up against the boulder. For one moment he tried to bring it back: her smooth body against his own. But all he could feel now was the stone.

His skin prickled. It was like electricity coming through the rock – through his shoulders and down his arms, into his chest, his groin, into his feet and back up into his face, which burned with it.

Momentum. Forward motion. The energy of the boulder's fall, now finding new conduits. It kicked him again towards the house, with all that rolling motion in his guts.

His reflection faced him in the patio door, standing against the pale shapes of the furniture inside. Such an indulgent expanse of glass. Her parents' delight.

He picked up a heavy plant pot and threw it. The glass shivered and came down like water. Easy.

The alarm whooped around his ears. But Dan moved steadily, confidently. Nothing could stop him. He was carried by gravity, down through the white spaces of the house. This was the ancient route of boulders; they had always come this way, long before houses. The building was fragile, paper and glass. As he walked he raised his hands and let them trail against things on the shelves, picture frames and vases falling left and right. What broke he couldn't really say; he didn't look back, but he felt that the whole house was coming down behind him.

He touched the front door and it fell open. He went out into the sunlight, over the front lawn and the two lanes of the road and the seawall, and then down onto the white sand of the beach.

Already he heard the sirens of the security guards, but he knew he was safe; he could not be stopped.

Dan walked down the beach until he was out of sight of the house. The dogs ran with him, looping down to snap at the breakers; one pushed a muzzle into the palm of his hand. He fussed over them, rubbing their ears and the wet fur on their chests. Then they left him, chasing each other back along the sand.

That was okay, he'd be all right. He'd make his own way home. But first, he reached down to take a handful of fine sand and put it in his pocket, to take away with him. It's what you did when you went on holiday to the sea.

HOMING

Before, it had always been a good road. Never big or busy, but alive, with an open feel despite the cul-de-sac. Ray and Nona's house took up one side, and opposite them was a sports field, ringed by shaggy eucalyptus trees. Unusual, fortunate, to have so much green space in the middle of town. People came past all the time: dog walkers, soccer players, domestic workers taking the short cut down to the taxi rank. Somewhere among the houses on the far side of the field, a man kept homing pigeons. In the evenings you could hear his looping whistle and see the flock turning, specks against the blue of Table Mountain. Nona and Ray always listened for the birdman's call.

At the end of the road was the face-brick retirement home. 'Look at the oldies,' Ray said, watching through their kitchen window as a posse of ancient women – and one man – ventured out from the home. It was a short walk down to the shops on the main road.

'Don't laugh. That's us, all too soon,' said Nona.

'Doesn't bother me,' said Ray. 'Potter down to the shops, read the newspaper, have a cup of tea. Looks all right.'

This was pretty much their schedule anyway. Nona was in her early sixties, Ray five years older. She'd done secretarial work, and he'd been a health and safety inspector, but that was all in the past now. Although they were both in good health, it was easy to imagine the years ahead, living where they did. One day, she and Ray would pack a small overnight bag, close the door behind them and simply walk up the road, into old age. And he was right: it wouldn't be so bad. They'd stroll around the field in the evenings, arm in arm. She wasn't ready for it yet, but she was also not afraid.

And so it was upsetting when the retirement home closed down. Ray and Nona read the news in the paper, but by then it was a done deal. Overnight, all the residents were bussed out to bigger institutions in the bleak northern suburbs, far from the old part of town. The place stood vacant for barely a week before the workmen arrived, throwing up hoardings across the façade and also, shockingly, around the perimeter of the field. A high wall rose at amazing speed and was painted a peachy pink, and behind it there reared the pink backside of a new hotel. The noise of construction, which went on for months, was unbearable, but the greatest affronts were the size and fleshy colour of the thing. Set down like a giant monopoly piece, fatly overflowing its monopoly square, the hotel filled up the space where the retirement home had been, and then turned the corner in an L and filled the space directly opposite Ray and Nona's kitchen window, too. Brash, three storeys tall, and featureless except for a row of mirrored windows that faced them over the top of the new wall.

'Are they even allowed to do that?' asked Ray.

'They already did,' said Nona.

And at a stroke, the road was mortally wounded. Where they lived was now a dying blood vessel, cut off from circulation. Nobody rode a bicycle past Nona's kitchen window any more, nobody walked a dog. The birdman fell silent: the sky in which his flock had stirred had turned into pink-painted plaster. It was as if the tyres of the cars and the soles of all those feet had not worn down the street, but had in fact been what sustained it.

As the weeks wore on, the tar cracked and developed sunken patches. Dandelions grew between the pavement edging stones. No council workers came to clean, to clear the drains or fix the potholes: it seemed the road had been erased entirely from the city maps. In dying, it started to give off the sweetish, not unpleasant smell of living matter breaking down, like compost.

It had long been a habit of Nona's, a little game, to look around at the city and think: how long would it last, if people vanished overnight? How many months or years before the bush came back; before birds made nests in the office blocks, and troops of baboons started lifting chunks of tar from the road, and the place all fell to bits?

Not long, as it turned out, not long at all. A piece of the city – a corner, a house, a familiar view – could vanish in a heartbeat. Turn away, turn back, and it's gone, or changed beyond recognition.

The new wall remained flawless. The paint was good stuff: it did not flake or puff with damp. Everything else in the alley, however, was in decline.

What disturbed Ray and Nona most was the least material of things: the light. Mostly, the house was much darker than before. They noticed it in the mornings, when bars of pale gold used to drop through the kitchen window, illuminating the cornflakes and coaxing the two of them into the day. Now the road was an alleyway, sunken and dim. The sunlight still came, but at the wrong time, and from an unnatural direction – east in the evenings. The first time they noticed it, Ray went outside to investigate.

'It's the windows,' he called back into the house.

Nona joined him. The alleyway was strangely illuminated, as if with several weak spotlights. Indeed, it was the mirror-glass windows of the hotel, three storeys up, flashing sunset light directly down at them. The new hotel, it seemed, had stolen their sunrise, and had slipped them a counterfeit sunset in exchange. It was actually hot, and distressing.

'Well, that takes the cake,' she said. 'When it's not a dungeon out here, it's a bloody oven.' Her eyes were stinging from the light.

Ray said nothing, just fetched a stiff-bristled broom and started sweeping away the last of the sand left on the pavement by the builders.

'It would be baboons,' Nona explained once again. 'They're clever, and strong, and they've got fingers. Plus those teeth.'

'I disagree. Dogs. Dogs would rule. The pack instinct would take over.' Ray was almost horizontal on the deckchair as he spoke, staring at the sky, although there was less of that now than there had been. They'd taken to sitting out here in the alley in the oddly lit evenings, as if it were part of their property. No one else set foot here now.

'Well. Maybe, for a while. But the baboons would win out in the end. One on one, I'd put my money on a big boy baboon. Dogs are too soppy; half of them would pine away for their owners. They'd just lie down and die. And they wouldn't be able to open up tin cans and things.' Nona could picture this all quite clearly, and with a kind of satisfaction: the baboons roaming the aisles of the abandoned supermarkets, the ravening dogs locked outside. Baboon babies playing on her kitchen table.

'Okay,' conceded Ray. 'Maybe baboons – on the ground. But the pigeons would do fine too. They'd carry on as per normal.'

This was true. She liked that about birds. How they were adaptable, took advantage. Walls were no problem, they could use walls; but they could also coast right over them, if need be.

The deckchairs were Ray's idea. It seemed he was making his peace with the new lie of the land. But for Nona, although she took her place there next to him in the evenings, the resentment did not fade. Every glance at the bland pink wall was a small humiliation. She wondered if there were wealthy guests already in the rooms, behind the glare of the windows: German tourists, Brits or Americans. She stared at the panes quite frankly, confident that no one was looking back. Those windows were not watchful eyes. They were more like expensive sunglasses: whoever was behind them wouldn't care to gaze on Nona and Ray.

'Miss those birds,' said Ray, blinking up at what was left of the sky.

And then, one evening, the pigeons returned, a cloud of them, nine or ten, settling and separating into a row along the top of the boundary wall.

Ray saw them first, as he and Nona were eating an early dinner at the kitchen table.

'Look who's here!'

'What? Who?'

'The birds, the birds! The birdman's birds.'

'How can you tell?' Nona peered through the window. They looked like regular street pigeons to her. Or were they sleeker, with a pedigree shimmer to the wings? Especially finely sculpted heads and beaks?

Ray fetched bread crusts from the kitchen and hurried outside. The birds seemed to have been waiting for him: when the bread hit the ground, they descended, cooing and beating the air.

'Hungry,' said Ray.

'Nonsense. A pigeon will never starve.' Although who could say, she thought, with these fancy racing birds?

'And lost. They don't know the way home, with this blooming big wall here.'

'They're homing pigeons. They know the way.'

'No, they do get lost,' said Ray. 'I read about it. They have magnets in their heads, and they get ... I don't know, depolarised.' He brushed the last crumbs off his palms, thoughtful. 'Poor little buggers.'

Now, on schedule, came the light from above, that unnatural flash that hurt Nona's eyes. For a moment she sensed a great bird settling above them, a firebird with its wings outstretched.

'That's what it is,' Ray said. 'The light, the reflections. It's confusing them.'

'Well. They probably have lice. Or bird flu. They look a

little off.'

The next day, Ray went out and bought a big bag of bird-seed, and after that the pigeons came twice a day, which Nona thought was excessive. Mornings and evenings, they sat waiting for Ray in a row on the wall, raising their tails to defecate down its pink flank. At least, thought Nona, most of them faced the alleyway, shitting judiciously down onto hotel property, too.

They read in the Tonight section of the *Cape Argus* that it was a luxurious place, patronised by politicians and celeb-rities, both local and international. Some evenings, they could hear the revels: laughter, music. On one occasion, fireworks. But none of this gaiety spilled over onto Ray and Nona. The pink wall dammed it up, diverted it like water, leaving them dry. All they got was the coloured glaze of party lights reflected in the windows, and the vibrations of popu-lar songs through the bricks.

Nona moaned about the noise going on till all hours. Ray didn't seem to mind so much, or even to notice. Twice a day the birds came to his feet, and he fed them. Nona, though, felt on edge, distracted by the flare of the evening sunlight and then the shadow that followed. Even as the hotel lit up for the evening, gloom gathered at the base of the wall and flooded the alley to its mouth.

What she did not confess to Ray was how the pulse of the music excited her – even prone on the ratty deckchair, on the shady side of the wall, among the dandelions and pigeon crap. It made her shift and sit up, straining to deci-pher the noises. Shrieks of pleasure. Crashes, laughter. Girl pushed in the pool? Smashed champagne glass? Some sounds were clearer than others. Once, sitting there beside Ray, she heard the distinctive pop and fizz of a champagne bottle, and then – miraculous – a cork came flying over the wall and landed right in her lap. She turned to Ray, eyes wide. But he was half asleep and had not seen. She gripped the cork with her fingernails, digging them deep.

Nona had to walk all the way around a surprisingly large and irregular block to get to the hotel entrance. As well as the playing field and the retirement home, several other small streets and properties seemed to have surrendered to the hotel grounds. She followed the boundary wall as it crooked left and right, at times trailing a hand on its high-quality matte surface, guessing at what it might conceal. What was the meaning of each swell and dip? What palatial amenities – indoor swimming pool, putting green, tropical glasshouse – could require these annexes and niches, this complex outline? It was impossible, now, to recall what had been there before.

It was noon when she came out onto the main road, holding her small bag close, and followed the wall along a last straight run to the entrance. It was a grand, curlicued wrought-iron thing, painted glossy black. The guard seemed surprised to see a human being on foot at the gates, but opened them a crack to let her through.

From the entrance ran an avenue of palms. Ahead, the building was indistinct: a shimmer of pink, the suggestion of steps ascending. The palms had not been there before, nor could they have grown so fast. They must've been transported whole from somewhere else, and then stuck into the soil like candles on a birthday cake. Nona remembered seeing a fully grown palm tree travelling down the road some months before: the bole laid flat on the truck bed like a giant's body on a bier.

She proceeded up the avenue, glancing side to side at the tended lawns, the cool greens and whites of the flowerbeds, the dappled light. There were very few people around. A gardener in green overalls stood motionless by a wheelbarrow, and a couple of tennis players patted a ball to and fro on a clay court in the distance. The air felt expensive in here, and easy on the lungs: more richly freighted with oxygen, perhaps. How could this all fit into what had been a small field, a block of flats, a modest neighbourhood?

Luxury, ease, light; it was disorientating, even exhausting. The avenue was longer than it seemed, and it felt like she was journeying miles, a pilgrimage, with only the grass-scented air to sustain her. By the time she reached the white marble steps leading up to the entrance, Nona might as well have been down on her stockinged knees.

Once inside the glass-fronted lobby, though, things speeded up marvellously. As if on a gentle swell, she was floated into the hotel, to beach at the front desk – a long bank of smooth wood just the right height for weary elbows. The light was subdued, and on the back wall a bank of keys with brass tags gleamed like a dragon's flank in a cave. Between this glimmer and the desk there flitted red-coated shadows, attentive, diffident.

A young woman with dark eyes, dark polished skin and a red tuxedo jacket came forward, tilting her head.

'I called yesterday,' Nona said. 'I have a booking. Single room. Your special.'

The carpeted foyer damped her words and made them

unconvincing. Nonetheless, they had a magical effect. The young woman found her booking and received her credit card with a smile – as if it happened every day, as if one did this all the time – then handed her one of the brass-fobbed keys like a winning ticket. Number twenty-three.

Nona found herself smoothly transferred into the care of a slim youth with neatly braided hair, the male twin of the receptionist. Polite hands lifted her bag, and she was conducted through the cool embrace of the elevator doors, up to a higher realm, and out into a corridor that seemed to her unaccustomed eyes to be carpeted in gold. Although the young man held her bag and not her arm, Nona had the feeling of being intimately escorted. She was tired, but she barely needed to lift her legs; the wondrous carpet flew her to door twenty-three, which fell away to admit her. And then the bellhop had withdrawn, and the door had closed soundlessly behind her, and she was kicking off her shoes and falling across a bed as crisp and cool as a drift of foreign snow.

Some time later, she arose and took a turn around her room, inspecting the surfaces, the knobs and drawers. She and Ray had only ever stayed in rundown country hotels, two-star affairs, or campsites. She fingered the fruit arrangement, peeked into the minibar and examined the bonbon placed on the pillow. It was all strange and extravagant: this lavish provisioning, so blindly generous. Rare gifts, for anyone with a key.

Through the window, sky. Nona opened the frame a crack and leant out, but felt no change. The air outside, clean and bright, was of a piece with the conditioned air that filled the room. She looked down.

And there it was. Three storeys below, beyond a strip of garden and just visible over the top of the boundary wall: the alley, the house, the pigeons. The wall cut off half the road from view, and only one empty deckchair was visible.

From this unfamiliar angle, she saw that the windows of their house were too small, and unevenly placed. A couple were cracked. You could see the plumbing on the back wall, with a nasty stain spreading from one pipe. Down on the ground, at home, she never noticed these things, but with height and distance the blemishes pulled into focus. It was shameful; repulsive, even. She felt a hotel guest's resentment of this disappointing view.

The pigeons – diligent heads bent, tapping away – made variegated patterns on the tar. Black and grey and white and mauve, each bird unique. They seemed to feed in silence: the clicks of claws and beaks were sounds too delicate to reach her.

Now something else, a blunt grey knob, pushed into the frame. It was her husband's head, surprisingly thin on top, inclined towards the birds. An intimate view. Almost embarrassing – like seeing the bare feet or buttocks of a dignified stranger. An arm was extended, in its frayed, familiar cardigan sleeve. After a moment, a bird hopped onto Ray's wrist. He seemed absorbed.

Seeing him from this unfamiliar angle, exposed as he was, Nona felt rebuked. She'd lied to him about this weekend, as she'd seldom lied in her married life. She'd used money from her own small savings to pay for the room, and told Ray that she was off to visit her sister. Now the cost seemed much greater than it had when she'd cut out the ad for the two-night special, or slid the credit card over the desk. These were pleasures owed to him, she knew. Poor Ray! So little luxury in his life!

But at the time of her decision – that champagne cork still slightly damp in her palm – some action had seemed urgently required.

And perhaps he was glad that she'd gone, that she wasn't there to disquiet him with her sighs and carping, her impatient rustling of the newspaper.

She dropped her eyes. Immediately below her window, peppermint grass flowed thickly to the base of the wall. There were parasols and camellia bushes and white garden furniture. You might sit down there of an evening, sipping a chilled drink, and never guess at what lay just an arm's length away, on the shabbier side of the wall.

Yet another attentive shadow in a red jacket appeared beside her garden chair, this one with a drinks menu. Everyone working here was young and unobtrusively attractive: eyes that took note but did not linger, voices low, manner deferential yet flirtatious to a finely judged degree. The waiter leant forward, showing her the tops of his long eyelashes.

'Gin and tonic, why not?' she said.

All at once, Nona felt happy again. The ease was back, the sense of smooth movement, although she was sitting quite still – at the heart, in fact, of a profound stillness. She and Ray, she saw, lived backstage to a perfect piece of theatre. The lighting in the garden was impeccable: even and mellow, unaffected by the alleyway's brassy reversals of glare and gloom. The only sound was a precise ticking in the air: the piston spritz of unseen sprinklers, or perhaps it was the hushed beat of luxury itself. The gin appeared, in a tumbler chocked with ice. She sipped, and felt the coolness trickling down into her belly.

Some things weren't controlled, however. There were white and olive streaks on the battlements: sure enough, the pigeons had left their mark on this side of the wall as on the other. And across the table top, a line of ants negotiated the crevasses and cul-de-sacs of the lacy metal to a spill of sugar at its centre. She imagined, warmly, their tiny ant amazement at this manna. They made her think of Ray: their earnest, uncomplaining labour, their focus on the small satisfactions before them.

She bent down to trace the line of insects to its source. It disappeared into the lawn, and emerged again to doodle up the corner of a flower planter, along its edge and through a tiny crack at the base of the wall. So: lowlife ants from the wrong side, smuggling out the loot. Again she wondered: how long? For ants and birds and grassroots to level this wall again, speck by speck, to break open the path that had been blocked?

But she didn't really want the wall broken down. What she wanted was for it to draw open and enclose her husband, their house, their life – put them on the right side, within this charmed perimeter of sugar and gin and shade.

She drank steadily, watching the ants come and go. Her glass emptied, and was filled. The evening light dimmed, while high above, the windows of the hotel started to shine – the angle oblique, the light more forgiving than it was at home. Small globes flickered on in the shrubbery, and the wall was bathed in dapples of rose and amber. Between the lights, the dusk seemed to soften and expand, becoming capacious. Patio doors opened and walls dissolved, making space for music, trays of cocktails, waiters, guests – such guests! Their clothes were precious and their scent was rare. Women leant at elegant angles, calves taut above high heels. Men shouted with laughter, gloriously assured. Half a dozen languages licked at Nona's ears. More red-coated servers danced from the shadows, carrying ice buckets and bottle after bottle of champagne.

Nona did not speak to anyone. She was content at her table, letting the crowd wash around her. She tickled her lip with the silver bubbles in her constantly refreshed glass; she smiled at the delightful waiters. She kept half an eye on the wall, but in all the flow and movement it stayed where it was; it didn't crumble or sway. Nona and the wall were still.

Later she would barely remember leaving the party, finding her way inside, the walk along the hushed corridor. But she would retain the feel of everything: the textures of wallpaper, wood and carpet. (Had she stumbled?) All so rich and inviting, so lush to the touch. Was there a young man by her side, red-coated, bright-eyed, holding her arm? Perhaps. Certainly she felt accompanied, but it might've been the scented air of the place that was so solicitous, that took her weight and guided her hand to the proper door handle, that caused it to turn.

The night was a dream of surfaces, sheathing her, pressing her down: luxurious friction.

Nona did not usually sleep naked, or on her stomach, but that was how she awoke. She was in a cool, dark place. She discerned the firmness of an unfamiliar mattress, and then – out of one eye – the grey field of a curtained window. With some popping of vertebrae, she broke the bed's hold, rolled onto her back, wedged herself up against the pillows and took stock. The room was bleary and ruffled. Against the habits of a lifetime, her clothes were strewn on the floor. And there was something else: small but troubling shapes in the dimness beyond the foot of the bed. A breeze belled the curtain and something pushed through with a rustle.

She took a moment to let the scene develop. The curtains sucked back out against the open window, as if the air in the room were plumping up, and more grey light infused. Hunched figures were arranged on the sill, on the desk, on top of the standing lamp. Six, seven of them. A fidgeting crowd of small, dour spectators. At the foot of the bed, one shook out its wings impatiently, stepped side to side and ejected a splatter of white onto the duvet. The bloody pigeons! A laugh of surprise burst from her – but that sent a jolt of pain through her temples. Wincing, Nona leant over to the bedside table, poured herself a glass of water and drank deeply. The pigeons cooed and shuffled, turning their heads this way and that to follow her movements. In their small eyes, in their sideways but steady observation, she saw a husband's chastisement. She supposed she should shoo them back out, before they did any more damage, but she found herself transfixed. She'd never thought of birds' faces as expressive – or even as faces; more as carved heads set with bead eyes – but these ones certainly looked attentive. Expectant, almost. It made her giggle again, despite the headache.

More water. Next to the jug was a small dish holding two wrapped biscuits. Digestives – the kind that Ray enjoyed with his tea. She pulled the cellophane off one, but her stomach rejected the thought as soon as she got a whiff of its mealy sweetness. It broke in her fingers, and once there were crumbs in her hand it was only natural to throw them to the carpet for the birds. In an instant, the boldest bird had hopped down from the minibar, legs outstretched and wings braking. The others piled in. They were shades of the same grey, birds and carpet, but the jostling animals' colour was alive and various. Wings fanned and snaky heads jabbed at the crumbs. She broke up the second biscuit, clucking her tongue like Ray did when he communed with the birds.

A delightfully extravagant thought came to her: room service. The phone was to hand, right next to the bed. She ordered toast, coffee, aspirin. More toast.

When the knock came, she went to the door and opened it just a crack to take the tray, ignoring the waiter's smirk. As soon as he was definitely gone, she poked a hand out again to hang up the Do Not Disturb sign.

Crumbs on the carpet, on the credenza, on top of the TV cabinet, at the foot of the bed. Content, Nona poured herself a strong coffee and settled back against the pillows to watch.

More birds hustled in through the window, shouldering each other, flapping and squabbling. Their claws scraped and ticked excitedly on the veneer cabinets, snagged in the bedspread. Every now and then one lofted into the air, wings clapping, before climbing back down into the skirmish. The carpet seethed. Once again, Nona was the still point in a moving scene. Her eyes grew heavy. There was a dusty, sweet smell of feathers and bird shit in the room, and a restful coo and rustle. She drowsed.

She dreamt she was walking in the hotel, down a long

gold corridor, looking for a way through the building. A flight path. But there were no exits here, no clear routes. The birds were with her and they were trapped, battering up against glazed windows, winging down corridors into dead ends, tangling in elevator cables. She pushed at the walls with her hands, searching for secret doorways; but the hotel could not be unbuilt.

She woke and dozed, woke and dozed, drinking more water and using the bathroom. The birds were dozing too, perched on towel rack and headboard. She wanted to sleep with them for ever, suspended three storeys in the air.

It was late afternoon when she finally rose. The pigeons were gone, leaving only their feathers and the blots of their droppings.

Already she could see that the room – despite the soiling, the smell, the clothes on the floor – was shrugging off this brief habitation. When the carpet shook its nylon pelt, all trace of living things would be repelled. Soon the room would be dreaming again in its pristine blankness: thoughtless, faithless, without memory. Readying its cool, promiscuous surfaces for the next encounter.

She dressed quickly, packed her few things, put out a large tip for the cleaning lady and left the key in the door. Back down the corridor, into the elevator, across the carpeted entrance hall and out, avoiding the eyes of the red-jacket boys and girls.

She walked down the long avenue of palms, rustling and stirring, with their own wild tribes of birds lodged like seeds in the cracks between the fronds. The grounds did not seem so enormous to her now. In every direction – beyond the flickering mesh of the tennis-court fence, past the rose garden – there was a wedge of pink wall blocking the line of sight. She left through the gates and walked the long way round, back home. The sun was low. She was a block away when she heard the whistling. High and looping – not the birdman's, but still familiar. Funny, that you could recognise the voice in a whistle.

When she turned the last corner, Ray was out in the alley, head cocked to the sky, seed in his outstretched palm.

'Home early,' he said.

She put down her bag. 'Missed you, didn't I?'

'They didn't pitch up this morning.' He let the seed fall to the ground and wiped his hand on his trousers. Fretful, like an old man. 'Didn't come.'

'Oh, Ray. They'll be back,' she said, taking his arm. 'Those birds, they know which side their bread is buttered.'

She helped him into the deckchair and took her seat alongside. It was that time of evening, when the sun in the windows cast weak shadows at their feet.

'You think?' he asked.

'You'll see.'

And so they reclined, Nona and Ray, their backs to the new hotel, saying a few quiet words to each other off and on. They watched the road and then the sky, and then the road again. That old road, altered but familiar, stolen from them yet still theirs. Patient in the changing and mysterious light, they waited for the birds to find their way.

PORCELAIN

The pieces of broken pottery in the sand revealed themselves subtly. Marion tried to be patient, letting her eye pick out the particular shade of blue, dulled by a crust of sand and salt. She took small steps, eyes fixed on the ground, squatting for a closer look when soft colour glimmered up from between the stones and shells. Mostly, it turned out to be nothing more than a mussel shell, the surprisingly pure blue of its inside margin tricking the eye. So far, she'd found only five bits of porcelain.

She couldn't see the breakers from here. The beach sloped up quite steeply from the water, flattening out into this broad stretch of sand before entering the milkwood forest. Here, in a series of oval depressions, was where the high-tide debris of the Indian Ocean had gathered over centuries: cracked pieces of fine old porcelain along with sand-frosted bottlenecks and rubber flip-flops. Not a few old sailing ships had come to ruin off this part of the coast – Dutch, Portuguese, British, journeying eastwards or hurrying home, laden with fancy goods.

The china was dry and porous, the glaze worn off and the edges smoothed. Triangular shards, holding no trace of the fury of the waves that had shattered them. The pieces grew warm in her palm, and clicked against each other when she opened and closed her hand in time to her steps. She crouched to examine a piece of bone – slender and white, probably a gull's. Perhaps there were sailors' bones here too.

Standing too quickly, Marion was struck by a sudden dizziness, as if the world were surging backwards, or as if her own life had sped up for an instant; but it was only the cold wind quickening. She stood still, waiting for this little tremor, this moment of imbalance, to pass.

An observer would see a tall, full-bodied young woman with a pink-and-cream complexion, her coarse hair twisted up and caught in a tortoiseshell clip. Her cheeks were flushed and her brown eyes clear. The hands cupped around her finds were dimpled and pink and slightly blotched in the cold, and the tapering fingers delicate. Hers was not a modern beauty. Marion looked like the women carved on prows of old ships: the heart-shaped face, the creamy bosom, the small mouth with its rose-petal lips, the classical nose. Looks that would have aroused admiration two or three centuries before. As if to enhance this impression, she was given to wearing layers of lace and corduroy, long dresses and blouses with low bodices to show off her neck and cleavage.

They were impractical clothes for beach walking: the hem of her skirt was crumbed with grit, and the dark-red crocheted shawl draped around her shoulders was damp at one end.

The wind picked up, strafing her cheeks with sand. She pulled the shawl across her face, her other hand closing around the porcelain chips. Then the cold rain came in from the sea, wetting her through and tightening her clothes against her breasts and thighs. She started to trot towards the trees, skipping awkwardly in the damp skirt, gasping with pleasure. She was young enough to be sped along, without warning, by such moments of animal exhilaration.

Breathless, she peeked into her palm, where the blue-and-white china gleamed. The rain had washed away the dullness. It was bluer than new, as if the pigment were still wet, the glaze just applied. As if it did not know that it had been mortally damaged, its pieces scattered and lost.

She allowed the squally wind to pull her up the beach and along the gravel road, towards the old wooden house that stood beyond the milkwoods. Pausing just before the veils of rain obscured the view completely, she saw, far out on the horizon, the faint suggestion of a ship – just a hint of tall masts, misty shreds of sails unfurling, palest smoke on pearl. Eyes closed, she put her head back and gave her neck and chest to the rain. When she looked again the ship had dissolved into cloud, but she stood for another minute or two in the downpour, staring out.

The wet steamed off her in the fire-lit house, where the walls were festooned with dry seaweed and strings of sea-urchin shells. Amelia, Marion's aunt, was sitting in her swivel chair at the trestle table in the corner, glueing together the pieces of a vase. She scowled through her spectacles, their mauve plastic frames clashing with her brown eyes.

Aunt Amelia had a special technique: she would fashion

an armature out of chicken wire, vase-shaped, onto which she fastened the broken bits of china with Prestik – a lark here, a pagoda there, two lovers on a bridge. So fragile, these ghostly vases, more air than porcelain. All around her, arranged on shelves and bookcases and table tops and in big woven baskets on the floor, were other pieces and assemblages: piles of shards, cracked plates with triangular bites taken out of their rims, undone jigsaw puzzles of smashed china.

'I saw the ghost ship,' Marion said, unwinding the damp shawl from around her neck.

Aunt Amelia held up angled tweezer-tips and gave Marion a keen glance. 'Did you really?'

Marion looked into the round mirror on the wall. She understood at once what had given Amelia that apprehensive look. In the mirror she saw not her own face, but her mother's: high colour in the cheeks, bright hair darkened with dampness that could be rain or sweat, eyes glowing as if they were melting in her face. Marion quickly looked away.

'No, of course not *really*, Auntie A. It was just the cloud coming in.' She went towards her aunt with her hands cupped together.

'Ooh, what have you got for me?' Amelia swivelled in the chair. She was in her late fifties, compactly built, although rounded and busty like all the women in the family. Despite the rainy weather, she was dressed as always in a loose short-sleeved shirt, khaki shorts and leather sandals. An outdoors woman: her calves were muscular and her biceps tight, beneath skin that was crinkled from years of solitary beach-walking. Hair that had once been gold was greying now, cut short every month with the kitchen scissors by

Auntie Belle. As a result it always looked a little tufty, with an irregular fringe.

Marion unclasped her fingers and let the chips of blue and white trickle off her palm and onto the table. They were still slightly damp.

'A good haul,' Amelia said intently. The gleaming points of her tweezers, like a fussy beak, teased apart the five shards. One with a tight geometric pattern, mesh-like; two plain white; one white with a narrow double band of navy; and the last, the smallest, showing the roof of a tiny pagoda.

'Will they fit?' asked Marion.

'Hard to tell ...' Amelia turned the pagoda fragment with the tips of the tweezers, flipping it over. 'This one – possibly ...'

Amelia was absorbed. Marion retreated to sit cross-legged in front of the fire, watching her aunt sort through the pieces that lay heaped on the table and in the woven bowls at her feet.

A few moments later, Marion heard footsteps behind her and felt firm fingers on the crown of her head. She twisted around to smile up at her other aunt.

'Hello, Auntie B.'

Aunt Belle took a hairbrush down from the mantelpiece and started to untangle Marion's damp hair, teasing out the knots. 'Such beautiful hair,' she said.

Belle was the second-oldest sister. She was less physically toughened than Amelia, softer around the middle. Her face was rounded, her upper arms fleshy and a little sagging. But the two women had the same clear brown eyes, the same air of vigour and resourcefulness. Belle was also dressed in a practical uniform of sandals, loose shirt and slacks, her silvering hair cut into a neat pageboy bob – the result of Amelia's painstaking handiwork with the scissors. Belle did not share her sister's fascination with smashed china. New pots were her thing. She enjoyed the company of the women in the village, where she ran a craft workshop: local women brought their clay pots to be fired in her kiln, and she arranged for the wares to be transported to town and sold to tourists.

There had been three sisters, all raised in this wooden house, all buxom and bright-haired. Amelia had helped their father, a GP, in his practice until his death, then later had volunteered at a veterinary clinic. Belle had been a social worker in the town before getting involved in the craft project. Neither of them had ever lived more than an hour's drive from the beach.

Of three sisters, only two now remained. Marion's mother had been the youngest and prettiest, a brilliant child, but not strong. Despite her vital appearance, Celia had been secretly fragile.

When Celia was only nineteen, Amelia and Belle had started to lose her. So careless. While they were busy on their energetic projects, their younger sister had floated away to the city. There she'd studied drama, sung cabaret, had love affairs, produced a child before she was twenty-three. She'd return to the beach house every now and then – always sparkling, always bringing too many gifts. But the soft sea mists had dimmed Celia's shine. When her mood darkened, she would leave at once, which meant she never stayed for long. Over the years, she visited her sisters less and less.

And in the city, with its late nights and loud days, its

electric light and shadow, Celia had started to separate. Her highs had become towering, her lows abysmal, until there'd been little left in between. Gradually she'd got lost in the troughs and ridges, the heavy waves of her illness – an illness that had probably always been in her, but that her sisters had not recognised until Celia was far, far out on a dark sea.

And Marion was with her, most of the time. When Celia was feeling good, the days were bright: she'd take her daughter shopping. She loved pretty things – ornaments, bric-a-brac. Often, these breakables were the things her hand fell to first when the mood shifted. She liked to throw things. Celia's frenzies of destruction were operatic, terrifying. Marion – aged six, seven, nine – rode them out. She would hide behind the couch or under the bed, barely breathing, waiting for the fit to pass. This was repeated many times, with accelerating rage, until, by the end, almost everything fragile in the house had been destroyed.

When things were quiet again, Marion would bring her mother tea and aspirin in bed.

Celia tried. She sent the little girl back to the aunts when she could. Marion spent school holidays and long weekends in the house by the sea; also, the two occasions when Celia was hospitalised. Each time, Marion felt a guilty buoyancy in being away from her mother, released from her duty of watchfulness. Later on, the beach house was where she went for her boarding-school holidays, and where she lived for her first year out of school. By then, guilt was part of the complex taste of the place, like the salt in the air.

Marion had been with her aunts when the news came. It was when she was eleven. Although the details were never discussed with her, she knew that her mother's death had been no accident. Celia had been just strong enough to make her own exit.

She was aware of how much she physically resembled Celia; how she too could fly into moods and rages and transports of exuberance, fits of tears or laughter. And she knew how her turbulence provoked her kind aunts, how it summoned anxiety into their eyes. They were vigilant, watching for cracks; for the signs they'd missed in Celia. And so Marion tried to be placid and cheerful, to gentle their suspicions. She hated it when they went still and watchful around her. It made her restless; made her miss her own life back home. In Cape Town she worked as a vet's assistant, just like her Aunt Amelia. Out here, on this emptier shore, she missed the incurious gaze of the animals.

'Why do you want to go back to the city, sweetheart? The sea air is good for you. Look at the colour in your cheeks,' said Belle. A quick glance from Amelia, over the mauve rims.

Marion sat still, keeping her head motionless as the brush tugged at her hair, suppressing the impulse to leap to her feet and shake out her hair with a shout, to kick and jump about. As a child she'd hated having her hair done, hated the enforced stillness every morning as Celia hacked at the knots with a comb, the tugs painfully communicating her mother's own frustration.

'Leave the child, Belle, for heaven's sake. She'll go if she goes and she'll stay if she stays.'

'What's in the city? Greed and grief, that's what. Greed and grief.'

Belle had worked out the knots now. The brush made a few last passes through the damp hair, and then Marion could feel her aunt nimbly separating three handfuls, the weight lifting away from her nape as the strands were braided together and secured. The tight sensation at the base of the plait was pleasurable. She was calmed, like a groomed horse.

And sitting here by the fire, watching the rain beating at the milkwoods outside the window, one mad gull spinning high up in the turbulent air, Marion did indeed feel safe – in the warmth of her aunts' affection, in this house that her grandfather had built for his daughters. She wanted to be in here with them, not out in the storm. Perhaps it might be possible to stay for good this time.

Behind her, Amelia sighed with satisfaction. '*Voilà!*'

Marion turned to see her positioning a piece on the framework of the phantom vase. It floated there, bellying out the lost curve.

'Well done, Auntie A! You got a fit.' Marion stood and went to her, reaching out to touch the vase.

'Careful,' said Amelia, and Marion smiled. After storm and wreck and tidal grinding, now to treat it like crystal. But she was careful.

'You'll never find all the pieces, surely?'

'Of course not. That's not the point. This isn't a jigsaw. But we can make it more whole than it was.'

'You and your old pots!' Belle snorted, pinching hair out of the brush. 'Spoils of empire, that's what they are. Flotsam of greed and conquest!'

Amelia directed a private smile at her floating vase and pressed the abutting pieces more snugly together. 'But still, very pretty,' she murmured.

'Rubbish. Why don't you collect the local pottery,

Amelia? Now that's beautiful. And useful.'

'Stop fighting, you two,' said Marion. It was an old argument, and the aunts were enjoying themselves. In this house, nobody raised their voices in earnest – not any more.

'Oh, don't go back to the city, darling child,' Belle sighed, laying a hand on Marion's smoothed hair. Marion knew that she was thinking of storms and disaster, greed and grief. But her aunt sounded resigned, as one is resigned to history.

That night, Marion dreamt again the dream of her mother: her young and beautiful mother, burning, throwing again and again a clear glass vase against the wall of the bedroom. Marion woke with the shattering all around her. It took a moment or two for her ears to clear, her heart to still; to hear only the quiet of the night, with its distant hushing of waves.

In the dream it was always that one particular vase, turning and turning through the air, while around her mother's tall, ecstatic figure the room was filled with sparkling splinters and a constant grinding sound of breakage that never seemed to slacken or to cease.

One ordinary evening two weeks before, Marion had taken each of her twelve good dinner plates – plain white china, which she had desired and saved up for and bought precisely because of their blank purity, the only complete set of crockery she'd ever owned – and thrown them, one by one, at the wall of her flat. For no real reason. A bad day in a bad week. A fight at work, a phone call from an old boyfriend. Not really reasons at all. It had frightened her, had made her feel that she was standing on the edge of a cliff, hurling her possessions into the void. In a way she was still standing there, waiting for the sound of them hitting the bottom.

It was this incident that had brought her back to her aunts, to the peace of this old house, as consternation had often done in the past. Although never before had she done something so alarmingly futile.

None of this could she tell the aunts. To tell them would be to confirm all their fears; it would force them to make some terrible gesture of recognition. But although she'd said nothing, still they seemed to sense that danger had touched her, that she'd fled to them from some pursuing shadow. This visit, the aunts had been particularly solicitous – watchful, kind.

But in her heart, Marion knew it had not been real. Yes, her wrist had flicked and the plates had spun from her hand, hair whipping across her cheeks and colour flushing the skin. But even as she'd acted out her mother's mad ballet – performed so many times, long ago in another small apartment, when Celia was not much older than Marion was now – she hadn't truly believed. She had never felt the weight of authentic madness under her arousal.

And afterwards, standing there with her bare feet, nicked and a little bloody, in the heap of shattered porcelain, she'd known that it had been an experiment. Drawing blood from the perfect skin inherited from her mother, cutting it to find what was inside. She had not entered the fury, had not been lifted away. And with the small wash of relief she'd felt at the ordinariness of her emotions – embarrassment, fright – there'd been a tickle of something else: maybe shame.

And so she must continue. She must allow Auntie B to brush out her hair as she had once brushed Celia's; she must go down to the sea and collect for Auntie A the pieces of broken plates and bowls. She must be serene, and so persuade them that Celia's heart had found in her own generous breast a peaceful resting place.

In the morning, when she was packing the car, Amelia and Belle came out to say goodbye. They presented her with a large cardboard box.

'If you have to go, take a little something with you,' said Belle.

Marion knew what it was: a clay pot from the village. Marion's flat was full of such gifts.

Driving back along the dirt road, she passed through the village and saw the women walking in twos and threes between the rondavels and the pink-plastered hexagonal houses, carrying paraffin tins and plastic drums on their heads. Not porcelain or clay, but functional. They made pottery for tourists, but for fetching their water, they used what worked best.

Back home in the city, Marion opened the cardboard box and found not a clay pot but Amelia's partially reassembled vase. It was carefully bound up in thin sheets of foam rubber and sticky-tape. She took it gently out of its wrappings and placed it on the dresser.

'Auntie A, it's beautiful,' she said on the telephone.

'It's just an old broken thing,' said Amelia, sounding pleased. 'Of course, half of it's still down at the bottom of the ocean.'

'But what if you find more pieces to fit?'

'Then you'll have to come and get them, won't you?'

After the phone call, Marion stood before the vase on the dresser for a long time. She had positioned it not centrally, but to one side. Next to it, invisible, was another, vanished vessel: the clear glass vase that used to stand on this same dresser when she was a little girl.

She touched the sides of the vase, the smooth patches of porcelain, the rough absences where the chicken wire showed through. And she was calmed by the feel of it. These broken pieces would not hurt her: spoils of empire, casualties of storm and wreckage, softened and blunted by time. Lovers on a bridge, a willow tree. And broken as it already was, she in turn could do the vase no further harm. Running her finger over the smoothed-off edges, she poked her fingertips into the gaps, feeling the parts that would always be missing, and the parts that were whole again.

STAR

Mrs Engelbrecht was not what you would call a sports fan. When her husband was alive, they'd followed the rugby, but she'd lost interest in TV in recent years. These days, she preferred to sit and play cards with herself on the balcony of her one-bedroom flat.

Not that there was much of a view. Long ago, you could see the sea, but that was before they built the Waterfront – and of course, now, the giant soccer stadium across the road. That was quite a business. The noise, the construction workers hanging around, the traffic! But, in truth, the neighbourhood had started changing many years before. So many new restaurants along the main road. Girls on the pavements at all hours, prostitutes she supposed; loud music from the corner bar. Mrs Engelbrecht never left the flat at night, it simply wasn't safe.

Bridge used to be the thing, but all those friends were gone, and so her game was patience now. Clock patience. She'd lay a ring of cards and play it through, then shuffle and deal them out again. There was no cause to feel alone. There was Luki, her dachshund, to keep her company. And Elizabeth, who lived down in the tiny basement storeroom and cleaned house for several of the residents, and who popped in most mornings. Mrs Engelbrecht could not afford to pay her much – but, then, there was very little to clean. The old lady barely ate, barely dented the mattress of her bed. At most, there was a film of milky tea left at the bottom of a cup, some crumbs of bread and cheese. Really, Elizabeth came to check that her employer was still there, that she had not fallen or faded away to nothing in the night. She would sit on the balcony and read the newspaper out loud to Mrs Engelbrecht, whose eyesight was no longer good, and then go on to her other char jobs.

Normally, they'd skip the sports section. But the upcoming World Cup was front-page news, and today there was a huge headline: a player from the French national squad had disappeared. There was speculation about hijacking, abduction.

'My word,' said Elizabeth. 'He was here – right here! They were practising here at the stadium, and then he was gone, just like that.'

'Well, really,' said Mrs Engelbrecht. 'I don't see why they're making such a fuss.'

'Because he's special,' said Elizabeth, reading. 'He's a big, big star. Look.' She folded the paper in two and held up the photo. A blurred face, a white smile.

'A black man,' observed Mrs Engelbrecht, who could not make out much more than that, what with her eyes.

'Ja,' said Elizabeth. 'But French.'

Mrs Engelbrecht clicked her tongue.

But Elizabeth would not let it be. She frowned at the picture and ran a dark thumb over it, a gesture halfway between a stroke and a rubbing-out. 'Maybe the skollies got him,' she said. 'Maybe they thought he was one of those Congolese.'

Mrs Engelbrecht clicked her tongue again. 'Poor chap,' she said, narrowing her eyes against the sun. Down below, she could see a crowd of people walking across the intersection, dressed in red: the colours of some team or other. They started singing, in ragged unison, halfway across.

'Ja,' said Elizabeth. 'Can you believe it?'

Mrs Engelbrecht left Luki's walk a bit late that evening – the streetlamps were already coming on. And such commotion: the foreigners milling, the mix of tongues in the bars with their doors flung open to the street. She kept Luki close and away from the louder bodies gusting past, who threatened to knock them right over, little old dog and lady both. They don't even see us, my girl, she thought.

Still, longstanding habit made her take Luki round the block to the old church, where the dachshund often did her business on a grassy corner, away from disapproving eyes. The lonely side street was darker than most. As she waited for the little dog to finish, she glanced over her shoulder.

'Come Luki,' she said sharply, tugging on the leash. Turning, she was startled by a flash of colour against the church stonework: lime green, shining in the light of the streetlamp. It was a man, slumped against the side of the building, half-hidden from view by a small flight of steps.

That in itself was not such an unusual sight, round here. Often one saw a homeless person, or a child, wrapped in a rough blanket and jammed in a corner to sleep, or someone half-dead from drink, a foot jutting out into the traffic. But Mrs Engelbrecht, who had been a nurse in her younger days, always felt uneasy about leaving a body lying; whenever she could, she would sidle closer, peering, trying to discern the rhythm of breathing. She considered herself a fine judge of states of consciousness.

With some stiffness, she bent herself over the supine form. He didn't look like a street person. He was too well-fleshed, his hair clipped short and neat. His clothes, she decided, were also too good. Some kind of silky top, track pants, bright white running shoes. There was a gold chain glinting at his collar. This man, she decided, was not drunk; she could smell nothing on him, no sweet fermenting odour. Nor was he completely well.

Luki touched the figure's cheek with a wet nose. The man moaned and turned away from the dog's kisses. His eyes came open, wet spots in the dark of his face. He had a long face with deep hollows under the cheekbones, a high fore-head. Black eyes under heavy, soft-looking lids. Perhaps it was those tragicomic eyes that made Mrs Engelbrecht think: French. He certainly did not look local. Too big, too dark.

She wrenched the dog away from the man's face. '*Sies*, Luki!'

The foreigner pushed himself upright, putting his back against the wall, and said something softly in a language she didn't understand.

'What's your name?' she tried. But he just stared up at her, unblinking. Trusting.

A bead of fresh blood leaked from his hairline, track-ing crookedly down into his right eyebrow. He winced and touched his head.

A vuvuzela blared again, closer this time; his shoulders jumped in fright, and then he laughed and exclaimed.

'What?'

'Football,' he said, smiling. He pressed one long-fingered hand to his chest. 'Me. Football.'

Mrs Engelbrecht sat the young man down on the edge of her bed. When she switched on the overhead light, he flared, vividly coloured. His shirt was not green at all but a fierce buttercup yellow; his skin was deep, deep black, his running shoes snowy. And his blood was extremely red. It was caked in his eyebrows and smeared on his shirt, across the number 7 on the front. Red fingerprints where he'd wiped his hands. He focused on her finger when she moved it left to right in front of his nose, although his gaze remained dreamy.

In her tiny bathroom, she filled a plastic ice-cream tub with warm water, clouding it with a dose of Dettol.

The Frenchman was up again by the time she got back to the bedroom, swaying on his feet. Luki was positioned in front of him. Mrs Engelbrecht, carrying the water, nearly tripped over the low-slung dog.

'Sit,' she said to the man. 'Show me.' She put the basin down on the bedside table. Then she gently reached up – he was tall – and pressed her soft old hands to his shoulders, manoeuvring him down again onto the bed. He sat with his hands flat on his thighs.

'Let me see.' Again she put her hands to his head, rolling his close-cropped skull forward. The wound sliced along the side of his skull and went behind his ear. It was quite deep at the back, bleeding down into his collar. Gently, with the damp corner of a face towel, she dabbed at the tender groove, cleaning it out. It looked like a knife cut, narrow and sharp-edged; but perhaps he had fallen against something. She squeezed a little Betadine ointment out onto her finger-tip, and he bent his head to her touch like an obedient child.

Luki had fetched her ball. It was a yellow plastic one from the supermarket, too big for her small jaws; she liked to nose it around the flat, bouncing it off walls and furniture. Now she rolled it forward, up against the man's feet, and stood waiting. He did not react. Mrs Engelbrecht saw that his eyes were closed.

'It's quite a deep cut,' she said, 'but you won't need stitches, I don't think.'

He kept his head bowed, his hands wound together between his knees.

'What happened?' she asked. 'Was it the skollies?' It was Elizabeth's word, not one that felt easy in her own mouth – not one that he would understand either, being French.

Disarmingly, he laughed, and then spoke a long, rapid sentence, opening his eyes wide.

'Take, take off,' she interrupted him. She mimed with exaggerated gestures for him to remove his shirt – then dropped her hands, embarrassed. She must look like a pale, ageing monkey, scratching in her armpits. But the man seemed to understand. He pulled at the back of his shirt, getting tangled up so she had to help it over his head. A waft of warm scent and sweat enveloped her face. He was lean, with a hard stomach and clearly defined arms. An athlete's body. There were no other wounds or scrapes on him. He gave her a smile, scratched an itch on his bare shoulder. Yes, she thought, he is European, you can tell. Something about the gestures. Quite elegant, really.

She pictured Elizabeth's face then. How angry she would be! How she would scold. This was the riskiest thing Mrs Engelbrecht had done for years.

'I'll make us a cup of tea,' she said.

She bundled the shirt up and took it through to the bathroom to soak. Seeing a red smear on her own hand, she thought then, distantly, of the risk: strange blood, infection. But what did that matter now, to an old woman?

When she brought the tea tray to the door, the man was sitting with his head down, slumped forward and sideways, as if he were slowly toppling over. She wondered how to approach, where to put the tray: the room was too small for all of them, Luki too. She felt suddenly exhausted.

'Luki,' she said. 'Shoo.'

The dog ignored her. Nudged the ball forward with her muzzle. It rolled, touched the tip of the man's white shoe. And this time, he lifted his head and observed the object in front of him. It was a little larger than a tennis ball, a little smaller than a bowling ball. He moved his foot, tapped it back to the dog. Luki gave an excited yap and pounced, and the toy skidded to the side. The foot came out, fetched the ball back into position.

And, suddenly, it looked different. It looked alive – but tamed, brought to heel. In one motion the young man stood and pulled back his foot. The ball followed. He inserted his toe under the curve of yellow plastic, and with a flick brought it up into the air, where it seemed to hang at chest level, awaiting instruction. He kept it suspended with a few playful taps off his knees. Tip, tap; he leant back and the ball ran across his chest, nagging at his shoulders; he ducked, and the ball came across his back, popped out behind his head and sat for a moment on his shoulder; then chased down his front onto the tip of his boot again. His mouth was slightly open, his eyes on the ball.

As she watched, Mrs Engelbrecht felt a rush of simple pleasure: such a show! In her house! And again and again, the ball looping, spinning, up and down, off the side of his foot, the toe, off his knee, off his …

'Your head!' she cried as the ball smacked broken skin.

He moaned and sat down hard – while the ball headed straight for the loaded tea tray.

For several suspended seconds, Mrs Engelbrecht performed her own gravity-taunting dance of balance and skill, the tea cups riding the listing deck, tinkling madly; she rocked back, then forward, and then at last, astonishingly, managed to land the tray safely on the foot of the bed. Losing control, as she did so, of the laughter that burst out of her like a girl's, spilling out over the trembling crockery. She laughed and laughed and could not stop, as the young man watched her with a dazed smile.

She persuaded him to lie down and covered him with a light blanket. He fell asleep almost immediately, sprawling diagonally on the old double bed with unselfconscious ease. She switched off the light and quietly closed the door.

Outside, on the balcony, she sat in her old wicker chair. Luki curled up in the chair opposite, which used to be Mr Engelbrecht's. Both of them were panting a little from the excitements of the evening. She calmed, and looked out into the night, over the crowds on the street, the rising laughter and revelry. Her gaze touched the top of that brand-new football stadium, settling into the dip of its roof. The joy she'd felt, watching the young athlete waltzing with the ball, had not left her. The feeling was the colour of the yellow shirt now hanging up to dry above the bath – throbbing and unreal, persisting at the back of the eye. And now it was combined with a sense of power. Ownership, spiced with a secret. That big new stadium was a nest, and she the child who'd climbed the tree and stolen the egg. The prize is here, in my house, sleeping in my bed, she thought. The star. And nobody knows.

In the morning – when she awoke on the couch, having slept very uncomfortably under a crocheted throw – she felt a niggling unease. All she could think of was that she had to return him somehow, like a lost dog or an overdue library book. And how would she go about it? She had no idea who to call. The police? The idea filled her immediately with guilt and fear. Perhaps she could just take him back to the new stadium, drop him off there at the tradesman's entrance? A riddle for someone to solve. Because of course – she saw now, in the daylight – she couldn't keep him.

First, though, she would make them some tea. They could sit outside on the balcony, watch the people pass below. She hesitated only briefly outside the door to the bedroom, then pushed it open.

The bed was empty, perfectly made up. Luki's ball positioned at its foot.

She hurried to the front door, saw that the bolts and chain had been loosened.

The doorknob turned in her hand and the door pushed open, nearly tumbling her backwards in fright. Elizabeth stood in the doorway, staring back at Mrs Engelbrecht in almost equal surprise.

'What's wrong, what's happened?' cried Elizabeth.

'What do you mean?'

'No, it's just, you look … your hair is all …' Elizabeth ran her hand over her own doek-covered head. She leant past Mrs Engelbrecht to peer inside the flat, frowning at the rumpled couch. 'Has someone been here?'

'No! No.' Mrs Engelbrecht steadied her voice. 'I'm feeling unwell. I didn't sleep. In fact I have a shocking headache.'

Elizabeth turned her severe gaze back to the old lady's face. 'Do you need the doctor?'

'Oh, good heavens, no. I just need a lie-down.' She applied suggestive pressure to the door. 'Perhaps I could ask you to come back tomorrow?'

Elizabeth resisted, pushing back and tapping a fingernail against the doorjamb.

'You sure.'

'Yes, positive.'

'Ja, okay. But I'm worried about you now.' Elizabeth turned to leave, suspicious.

Just as Mrs Engelbrecht was about to close the door, she noticed the morning paper tucked under Elizabeth's arm. 'Wait!' She reached out and plucked at it. 'Can I see that?'

'Do you want me to come in and read?'

'No, just … I wondered what happened. About the football player? That Frenchman.'

'Oh, that.' Elizabeth snorted in amusement. 'No, they found him. He'd passed out at some shebeen.' She made a tippling gesture with her cupped hand at her mouth. 'French!'

Mrs Engelbrecht went still, her fingers clamped to the page.

'They found him?'

'Ja – see for yourself. Yesterday afternoon already. Can you believe it?' Elizabeth lifted her arm, releasing the paper to Mrs Engelbrecht's fingers. The loose inside sections unfurled, the pages separating out and subsiding to the floor.

The panes of glass in the balcony doors shook lightly in their frames. Both women turned to look. An electronic whine lanced the air, and a voice addressed them. The voice of a hidden giant, it seemed: muted but huge, garbled, vaguely haranguing. Vibrating through walls and floor.

And despite it all, all this brash noise, Mrs Engelbrecht could feel last night's triumph, still warm in her chest. As if she'd been the one to kick the first ball of the tournament – and far, and high.

Then came rising strains of music: the anthem, they recognised. The roar of a multitude.

'World Cup,' said Elizabeth. 'Now it starts.'

THE BRONZE AGE

When we got there it wasn't much to look at, just the visitors'
centre and then a field with a grassy slope behind it. Three
hairy guys lounged at the entrance in sackcloth-type garments,
with bogus helmets and swords and shields – plywood and
bronze paint, I reckoned. I smiled as we passed, but they just
stared back at us, surly. Maybe they were staying in character.
Barbarians. Robbie kept his head down. He was such a shy
kid, easily cowed.

This was what I'd come for: to spend time with my boy.
A week in the UK wasn't cheap, but Gemma thought it would
be better than flying him to Joburg, less disruptive. It was
only four months since they'd left, after all; he needed to
get settled.

Gemma was worried. Robbie had been having a rough time
at the new school. Got a black eye, wouldn't tell her how. And
a couple of boys in his class had been caught with knives –
'They're only twelve!'

Jees, I thought. What kind of kak school did you stick him

in, Gem. The whole point had been to get him away from that kind of thing. That had been Gemma's mission, ever since they'd had that break-in last Christmas.

He just needs time with his dad, she said. Have a chat.

We didn't do so well with chats, me and Robs. At worst, they ended up with me shouting and him crying. I couldn't tolerate tears; this was one of the many things Gemma and I fought about, when we were still together. And Robbie didn't want to tell me things, not since the divorce. Certainly not since Gemma took him off to another country. Skype sessions were impossible, we'd found: both of us mute with awkwardness, avoiding webcam eye-contact at all costs.

So here I was, spending time. I'd even looked up 'kids activities' online, and found this place. A bronze-age burial site, a museum. It looked sedate and nerdy, not the kind of thing I would've been into at that age, but whatever. Gemma would approve. The plan was to ease us into the week, to prepare us both for the chat part.

In the visitors' centre there were display tables of gold coins and bits of copper jewellery and spear-heads, all dug out of the hill beyond, apparently. The barrow. I hadn't known this meaning of the word. They had a model of a bearded man in one corner, and he was the real deal: bronze breastplate, purple-dyed cloak and a fine big sword with a gleaming pommel. His head came only to my shoulder, even with the helmet. You couldn't make out a face behind the eye-slits.

'Wicked,' Robbie said.

He used the word tentatively – still trying out the accent. A lot of things were new to him, to us. Even getting to the place today: finding the bus, then the train, all that, instead of jumping in the car like we did back home. Where we came from, old things in the ground were not so grand. Stones, bones. Maybe some broken bottles. Things you could believe people had chucked away. Not like this stuff.

'No touching, Robs,' I said.

The little greying man who seemed to run the place was hovering behind us. 'He looks small but those chaps were very tough, very strong. When that blade was sharp, it'd take your head off!' He laughed. 'I'm Phillip, by the way.'

Robbie had moved on to a glass cabinet of human bones, including what looked to me like a teenager's skull: clean white curves delicately sutured together, strong teeth, fine jaw; and an ugly splintered hole right through the crown.

'Did that happen in a battle?' asked Robbie.

'Or murder!' said our guide. 'Ritual killing, could be, too.' Everything seemed to make him chuckle.

'Like, human sacrifice?'

'Indeed. Or a punishment. They executed thieves, for example.'

'How?'

It was the most Robbie had said all day. I smiled coldly at Phillip. We were supposed to be doing soothing, non-violent activities, after all.

'This one? Spear, most likely. Sometimes they brought out the old garotte.' He tugged his fists sideways across his neck, stuck out his tongue and rolled his eyes to demonstrate. 'We've seen cut throats, too. That sort of thing.'

'Wicked,' said Robbie again.

He was entranced. It was hard to tear him away to go outside for the planned activity, which I'd paid for. A crazy amount, if you did the rand/pound exchange in your head, which I was trying not to do.

They'd laid out a grid on the field with string, like a real archaeological dig. There was a bunch of kids waiting with their parents, in wellingtons and waterproofs, little trowels in their hands. I saw at once I'd made a mistake – Robbie was a year or two older than most of the children here.

'You want to do this?' I asked him softly. 'You don't have to.'

'No, I want to. It's interesting,' he said.

'Right,' said Phillip, 'now each of you choose a square to excavate. You put your soil in your sieve, shake it all around and see what pops out. Let's see who finds the treasure hoard!'

The kids dashed off like old-time prospectors to claim their patches. Robbie hung back, and eventually chose a square right in the far corner, away from the others. Not one to mingle.

'Ready, steady, dig!'

Some of the other parents had gone to hunker down next to their kids, but I didn't want to crowd Rob. 'What happens if they hit something valuable?' I asked Phillip. 'Who does it belong to?'

He smirked. 'Oh no, we choose the spot quite carefully. There's nothing in this part of the site. All the good stuff we've found was up in the barrow or beyond – the warrior's grave, the armour, the horse skeletons ... Down here they might turn up pieces of pottery, sheep bones, maybe the odd horseshoe. Sometimes we salt the place with a couple of goodies. A few old coins, nothing of great archaeological worth. The kids usually dig out a half-dozen bits and pieces – they love it, it's like finding the sixpence in the Christmas pudding. Then after lunch we have some swordplay.'

'Oh, that's what those guys were. In the costumes.'

'Yes, our reenactors. Bit of fighting, show the kids how to make fire with a flint, that sort of thing. They can have a go with the weapons, too. It's good fun.'

Right. Gemma would just love that. Take the kid out for the day, teach him some blade skills. Although, I considered, that's probably what my dad would have done for me, if I'd been bullied at school. At least he'd taught me how to punch. But Gemma wasn't having that, not then when we were a family, and certainly not now.

I took myself off to the side of the field to watch the kids dig, keeping my distance from the other parents.

It was a bleak place, really, with few interesting features. Just the bare side of a hill. I wondered how many skeletons were still in the barrow, under the grass; how much blood had soaked into the soil here over the centuries. It seemed a damp place to die. But maybe my mood was just low. I was watching Robbie. He didn't seem right. Hunched over on the ground, he looked frail, sweatshirt sleeves pulled down over thin wrists. I could see the faint bruise over his left eye, and felt a surge of rage for the savage little shits at his school. I was definitely not going to tell Gemma about the sword-fighting.

'Let me guess ... South African?' Phillip again, at my elbow.

'Got it.'

'Cape Town?'

'Joburg.'

'Ah!' he said. 'Rough place.'

'What?'

'I've heard stories. My wife's cousin got mugged in

Durban. Guy with a gun. They were just walking along the beach, minding their own business. Don't blame you for making the move.'

'You can get mugged anywhere,' I said, and turned away.

The other children didn't have Robbie's determination. They were digging slower and slower, and none of them had made much of an impression on the soil. A couple were giggling and prodding each other with their trowels. The older kids looked bored and I saw one of them playing with his phone. Only Robbie had his head down, working.

It was starting to rain lightly, and I was thinking of cutting things short and heading back to the station, when someone gave a shout – 'Got something! Look!'

Phillip hurried over to examine the find, holding it up for all to see. Didn't seem like much to me, just a piece of rough pottery, but the old boy was making a big show of excitement. The kids downed trowels and the other parents gathered round to have a look. I stayed back.

Robbie had pretty much demolished his square and was still digging deeper, with suspicious intensity. As I watched, he stopped short and stared for a moment, then put the trowel aside and reached carefully into the hole with both hands. He looked up at me, a shifty glance, and then away.

When I got over there, he was trying to cover something up. 'Go on, show me.'

Reluctantly he drew his hands away. More smashed pottery. This had been a biggish pot with a stippled pattern on it, and it looked like it had been whole until a few seconds ago. You could see the terracotta colour on the rims of the broken pieces, bright against the earthy brown of the exterior.

'I'm sorry,' he said, voice wobbling. 'It was an accident.

My spade just went straight through. Don't tell, Dad, please.'

I took a deep breath. 'Okay, Robs,' I said, keeping my voice down. 'It doesn't matter. It's not important. Stupid old pot.'

The guide was looking over at us. 'Something there?' he called.

I gave him a cheery wave. 'Nope, nothing. False alarm.'

I took the trowel and shoved the disturbed soil back over the broken pieces. 'Pot? What pot?' I was relieved to see my son smile.

Phillip had changed his outfit for the swordplay part of the afternoon. He looked like a pixie in his tapering silver helmet, a dab of luminous blue face-paint on each cheek. Behind him hovered a couple of the bearded chaps in their jerkins and tin armour.

'Are you joining in, young man?' he called over to Robbie. 'Shall I fix you up with a battle-axe? Pike? What's your weapon?'

'You ok, Robs?' I said. 'We don't have to stay.' But he was already stepping forward eagerly.

I was disconcerted. The day was stretching longer than I'd planned. I'd thought we'd be in the pub by now, me with a pint and Robs with a Coke, getting that big talk out of the way. I'd ask him how things were at school. Was he handling? Did he miss home? I'd show him the secret of how to make a fist, tell him not to tell his mom. Maybe let him have his first sip of beer.

But hours passed and he was still out there in the drizzle, spinning around with some sort of balsa-wood longsword in his hands, a look of ferocious concentration on his face while some bored extra parried disinterestedly with a plastic shield, clearly dying for a smoke.

I had to smile though. There was 'woad' smeared on Robbie's cheeks, so you couldn't see the bruise, and he looked so young, a little kid at a face-painting party, thrilled with transformation.

Robbie was tired on the train. He leaned against me in the seat like he used to do when he was a toddler. It wasn't really comfortable, but I let him rest.

'Hey Robs, don't mention to Mom you were playing with swords today, okay?'

He chuckled. 'She'd freak out.'

I relaxed a little. Maybe it wasn't really necessary to talk things through, not in so many words. Maybe this was enough: these moments of solidarity, a shared laugh, his shoulder pressed to mine.

I thought he'd fallen asleep, he was so still, but then he shot out a finger. 'Dad, look!'

It was a horse and rider, galloping parallel to the tracks, so fast they seem to be almost keeping pace with the train. A strange sight: the man was muscular, bare-chested despite the rain, and his long dirty-blond hair flew out behind him like a flag.

'Hey, it's one of those reenactors,' I said. 'Coming after us for revenge.'

But Robbie didn't laugh. He craned his neck to watch the rider drop from sight.

'I'm joking, my boy,' I said.

But all I could see of Robbie's face were the sharp angles of his jaw, his purpled cheekbone.

Later, we ate pizza and watched a bit of TV. Some reality show involving fit and half-naked guys and girls racing through an obstacle course. We were staying in my mate Gavin's house, while he was conveniently away at a conference. It was comfortable. Robbie ate a whole pizza by himself, chewing methodically, eyes on the screen. I watched his jaw working in the bluish glow. He seemed calm and absorbed, contented even. I waited for the programme to end before I turned down the sound and made my attempt: 'So, Robs.'

He stiffened.

Ah, screw it, I thought. 'Want to tell me what's been going on at school? How's things?'

One more chew, a swallow. 'Things are okay.'

'You made any friends?'

Shrug. 'Sure.'

'They the ones who gave you this?' I touched my own left cheekbone, under the eye.

He looked quickly up at me and then away, at the silent figures moving on the screen. 'I got that in football practice,' he said. 'I said to Mom.'

I watched him in silence for a moment. All the ease was gone, in a stroke. 'May I be excused?' he said politely.

It shocked me a bit, the cold little phrase.

'But it's still so early, buddy.' I couldn't remember what his bedtime was meant to be, these days.

Another shrug. 'I'm quite tired, actually.'

I let it go. 'Okay, Robs. See you in the morning.'

Later, I phoned Gemma and we talked quietly for bit. I missed that: telling her about my days. But she was mostly concerned with Robbie.

'Have you spoken to him?' she asked.

'A bit. Not really.'

'Mike …'

'I will. I will tomorrow.'

'Promise?'

'I promise.'

As I hung up, there was a cry of pain from the upstairs bedroom.

I rattled the handle until he unlocked the door. 'Jesus, Robbie!'

He didn't try to hide his hand, which was streaming blood down his wrist and onto the carpet. I dragged him to the bathroom and wrapped the hand in a towel. After a bit the bleeding stopped. We were both white with fright. Robbie had gone completely passive, and let me run water over the cut and pat it dry. It was clean and straight, right across the left palm.

I was angry, thinking, what the fuck am I going to say to Gemma about this.

'What the hell, Robbie? What did you do?'

'I was just playing,' he said, sounding out of breath. 'It was an accident.'

'Where is it. Where's the knife?'

It didn't take me too long to find it tucked away under his pillow, with bloody prints all over the slip.

It stopped me short.

It was a very beautiful thing.

Bronze handle, set with a flint blade. It looked extremely old but as fresh as the day it was made, the metal gleaming, the edge still sharp. I picked it up cautiously, weighed it in my hand for a moment. It was sticky with my son's blood.

I took it back to the bathroom where Robbie was sitting on the side of the bath, clutching the stained towel.

'Bloody hell, Robbie,' I said wearily, 'this was a fucking stupid thing to do.' I sat next to him and took his hand in mine, gentler this time, and unwrapped the towel. Not deep enough for stitches, I didn't think. I'd been a medic, back in the army in the old days, so I'd seen a bit, knew a bit. I found some gauze in the medicine cabinet and patched him up. The bandage looked like a boxer's mitt, the wrist even frailer than before. I rested his wrapped hand in mine and we both contemplated it for a moment.

'It was inside the pot,' he said.

'Right. So why did you take it?'

'I just wanted it. For school.'

'For school.'

'The other guys ...'

'Oh for god's sake Rob – the *guys*? The *other guys*? You want to get into it with those cretins? Get a knife in your gut? You want to know what that feels like?'

With a whimper he pulled his arm from me, cradling it to himself.

'Oh for Christ's sake, you will *not* start crying! You're twelve years old, you're not a baby.'

He went immediately silent. A stubborn set to his mouth.

'Look, we're taking it back tomorrow okay? It's a dangerous object. Probably illegal. And anyway, we don't take things that don't belong to us.'

'It doesn't belong to them either!' he burst out. 'That stupid old guy, why is it his? It actually belongs to a dead person!'

'It belongs to everybody. It should be in a museum. We're

going to take it back, and you're going to explain to them what you've done.'

'Please – please Dad, no.'

I held my breath, let it out in a sigh. 'Okay, look, it's late. We'll discuss it in the morning. Go to sleep now. I'm very tired and so are you.'

I took the knife with me upstairs. I was shaken. Picturing the blade going in, and all that blood.

I was woken much later by sounds outside: I could swear it was a horse, whinnying. In the neighbour's garden there seemed to be some kind of party going on, with people huddled around a fire. They weren't talking much. There was a pungent smell in the air, a bit like livestock, a bit like weed. One man, standing to the side, had his eyes on me. In the firelight I could see he was stocky guy in a leather vest, with a long beard knotted into a braid. Some kind of metal biker look. He said something, a single harsh syllable, and the other figures around the fire turned their heads to stare up at my window.

Then all at once he was running at the picket fence, slamming his body into it with a crash. Bounced back, and glared straight up at me again. Startled, I rammed down the window and stumbled against the bed, crouching out of sight.

What the fuck?

Looking down, I was startled to realise I'd been holding the flint knife the whole time. Was that what set him off? I pulled the duvet off the bed and took it downstairs to the couch in the lounge. I lay there wide awake, watching the front door, alert for trouble. But the night was quiet again.

I turned on a lamp and looked more closely at the knife. I used to collect knives when I was a teenager myself. Thought they were special then. And this one was a beauty; I understood why Robbie couldn't leave it behind. It sat well in the hand, heavy but perfectly weighted. Made you want to throw it in a clean arc, stick it deep. The flint blade was translucent, dappled grey. I wiped it off and buffed the handle with a corner of the duvet. The metal came up beautifully. Fine craftmanship: some kind of animal – a hunting dog maybe – worked in copper wire; dark red stones for eyes. I thought about keeping it for a minute, taking it home; but then I snorted. Let's see you get that through Heathrow security, china. It was an English knife and it was staying here.

I tucked the knife under the couch cushion and pushed my thoughts away from all that: airports, passport control, exit lounges. Goodbyes and separations.

In the morning I went out back to have a look over the fence into the adjoining garden. There was no one in sight, and certainly no horses. Surely a dream? But there was a blackened patch on the lawn and the flowerbed looked milled up. I should mention it to Gavin. Fucked-up metal-head neighbours.

Again, Robbie was quiet on the train, staring out the window. Steeling himself, I thought. Two pictures came to me: in one, we stayed on this train till London, and on to the airport, where in the arrivals hall I tossed the knife into the bin for overlarge shampoo bottles and nail-clippers. I took my son by the hand instead and pulled him through the gates, and through the air and all through the night back home, with me.

In the other, I took the knife and placed it in his hand, and showed him how to fold his fingers round the handle. So long, son. Look after yourself.

'Dad? Can I hold it?'

'Sure,' I said after just a moment's hesitation, and gave him the knife. It was important for him to be the one to give it back to the museum, I thought; for him to take responsibility for his actions. 'Just be careful with it, ok?'

He nodded and held it soberly in his lap for the rest of the journey, the blade in his bandaged palm. When we arrived at the visitors' centre, it was closed and there was nobody around. It seemed even more barren than before. I looked at the sweep of the field and saw nothing but a grid of squares, some of them lucky and some unlucky: treasure, graves, coins, knives, and no way of knowing which you'd land on.

A clashing sound, metal on metal, was coming from behind the hill.

I put out my hand to Robbie, although he was too old to take it. 'Throw the knife down anywhere, Robs. Let's get out of here.'

But he pulled away, his attention caught by something beyond me.

'Look,' he said. 'There. The men are over there.'

There was a figure up on the barrow, silhouetted against the morning sun. One of the reenactors, must be: he seemed to be leaning on a tall spear. I couldn't tell if he saw us, but he turned and disappeared over the rise.

'Robbie, wait –' but Robbie was already jogging up the hill. Knife in hand.

I went after him but I couldn't keep up; like an old man

I struggled and panted. I'd never seen Robbie run like that before: so purposeful. At last I reached the crest.

On the other side, an army on the eve of war.

I was looking down onto a broad, grassy hollow. Smoke from dozens of fires hung low on the ground, creeping between clusters of dun-coloured tents. Beyond, horses grazed, and everywhere men were busy, polishing armour, sharpening axes. A couple were sparring with swords, and I could hear shouted jokes and curses, though I couldn't make out the words. Breastplates and helmets glowed, reflecting warmly in the morning sun. It must be a particularly elaborate reenactment, some major battle, I thought.

Robbie was way ahead of me, already halfway down. I could not catch him up.

On the far side of the camp, a rider stood watch. He turned the head of his horse towards us. We were seen. And except for Robbie, every figure in the scene went still. Smoky light shivered, and things came up clear and sharp, like memories recovered in a dream. The smell of meat and woodsmoke pierced me, with a sharpness I had not felt since I was young. I saw the warriors' painted skin, their braided hair, the bright details of their armour; the keen edges to their blades. The scars of blows received on their shields and on their ancient faces. Those voices familiar yet strange, a language that maybe I used to know, a long time ago.

Robbie slowed, but kept going. They all saw him now. The warriors were quiet, as if they'd been waiting. The rider walked his horse forward into the open space. His face was concealed behind a shining visor. He raised a gauntleted hand, but I couldn't tell what that meant, greeting or threat. Robbie went to meet him, his body tiny before the massive armoured animal. But he held himself upright and looked straight ahead, hands by his sides, one wounded, the other with the blade.

And then he turned to look at me. The space between us was half a lifetime and half a world, was a thousand years. I put my hand to my face and there were tears. As if I'd cut myself.

POISON

Lynn had almost made it to the petrol station when her old Toyota ran dry on the highway. Lucky me, she thought as she pulled up onto the verge, seeing the red and yellow flags ahead, the logo on the tall façade. But it was hopeless, she realised, as soon as she saw the pile-up of cars on the forecourt. A man in blue overalls caught her eye and made a throat-slitting gesture with the side of his hand as she came walking up: no petrol here either.

There were twenty-odd stranded people, sitting in their cars or leaning against them. They glanced at her without expression before turning their eyes again towards the distant city. In a minibus taxi off to one side, a few travellers sat stiffly, bags on laps. Everyone was quiet, staring down the highway, back at what they'd all been driving away from.

An oily cloud hung over Cape Town, concealing Devil's Peak. It might have been a summer fire, except it was so black, so large. Even as they watched, it boiled up taller and taller into the sky, a plume twice as high as the mountain, leaning towards them like an evil genie.

As afternoon approached, the traffic thinned. Each time a car drew up, the little ceremony was the same: the crowd's eyes switching to the new arrival, the overalled man slicing his throat, the moment of blankness and then comprehension, eyes turning away. Some of the drivers just stood there, looking accusingly at the petrol pumps; others got back into their cars and sat for a while with their hands on the steering wheels, waiting for something to come to them. One man started up his BMW again immediately and headed off, only to coast to a halt a few hundred metres down the drag. He didn't even bother to pull over. Another car came in pushed by three sweating black men. Their forearms were pumped from exertion and they stood for a while with their hands hanging at their sides, exchanging words in isiXhosa with the petrol attendants. There was no traffic at all going into the city.

Over the previous two days, TV news had shown pictures of the N1 and N2 jam-packed for fifty kilometres out of town. It had taken a day for most people to realise the seriousness of the explosion; then everybody who could get out had done so. Now, Lynn supposed, lack of petrol was trapping people in town. She herself had left it terribly late, despite all the warnings. It was typical; she struggled to get things together. The first night she'd got drunk with friends. They'd sat up late in front of the TV, watching the unfolding news. The second night, she'd done the same, alone. On the morning of this, the third day, she'd woken up with a burning in the back of her throat so horrible that she understood it was no hangover, and that she had to move. By then, everybody she knew had already left.

People were growing fractious, splitting into tribes. The petrol attendants and the car pushers stood around the taxi. The attendants' body language was ostentatiously off-duty – ignoring the crowd, attending to their own emergency. One, a woman, bent her head into the taxi and addressed the driver in a low voice. He and the *gaardjie* were the only people who seemed relaxed; both were slouched low on the front seats, the driver's baseball cap tilted over his eyes. On the other side of the forecourt was a large Afrikaans family group that seemed to have been travelling in convoy: mother, father, a couple of substantial aunts and uncles, half a dozen blonde kids of different sizes. They had set up camp, cooler bags and folding chairs gathered around them. On their skins, Lynn could see speckles of black grime; everybody coming out of the city had picked up a coating of foul stuff, but on the white people it showed up worse. A group of what looked like students – tattoos, dreadlocks – sat in a silent line along the concrete base of the petrol pumps. One, a dark, barefoot girl with messy black hair down her back, kept springing to her feet and walking out into the road, swivelling this way and that with hands clamped in her armpits, then striding back. She reminded Lynn of herself, ten years earlier. Skinny, impatient. A fit-looking man in a tracksuit hopped out of a huge silver bakkie with *Adil's IT Bonanza* on its door and started pacing alertly back and forth. Eventually the man – Adil himself? – went over to the family group, squatted on his haunches and conferred.

Lynn stood alone, leaning against the glass wall of the petrol-station shop. The sun stewed in a dirty haze. She checked her cellphone, but the service had been down since the day before. Overloaded. There wasn't really anyone she wanted to call. The man in the blue overalls kept staring at her. He had a thin, villain's moustache, and seemed to be perspiring excessively: his face had a look of damp clay. She turned away.

The dark girl jumped up yet again and dashed into the road. A small red car with only one occupant was speeding towards them out of the smoky distance. The others went running out to join their friend, stringing themselves out across the highway to block the car's path. By the time Lynn thought about joining them, it was already too late; the young people had piled in and the car was driving on, wallowing, every window crammed with hands and faces. The girl gave the crowd a thumbs-up as they passed.

A group was clustering around one of the cars. Peering over a woman's shoulder, Lynn could see one of the burly uncles hunkered down in his shorts, expertly wielding a length of hose coming out of the fuel tank. The end was in his mouth. His cheeks hollowed; then with a practised jerk, stopping the spurt of petrol with his thumb, he whipped the hose away from his mouth and plunged it into a jerrycan. He looked up with tense, pale eyes.

'Any more?' he asked, too loud.

After a while, the group moved on to the next car.

Lynn went to sit inside, in the fried-egg smell of the cafeteria. The seats were red plastic, the table tops marbled yellow, just as she remembered them from childhood road-trips. Tomato sauce and mustard in squeezy plastic bottles, crusted around the nozzle. She was alone in the gloom of the place. There were racks of chips over the counter, shelves of sweets, display fridges. She pulled down two packets of chips, helped herself to a Coke and made her way to a window booth. She wished strongly for a beer. The sun came through the tinted glass in an end-of-the-world shade of pewter, but that was nothing new; that had always been the colour of the light in places like this.

Through the glass wall, she could see the petrol scavengers had filled up the tank of Adil's IT Bonanza. They'd taken the canopy off the bakkie to let more people climb on. The uncles and aunts sat around the edge, turning their broad backs on those left behind, with small children and bags piled in the middle and a couple of older children standing up, clinging to the cab. What she'd thought was a group had split: part of the white family was left behind on the tarmac, revealing itself as a young couple with a single toddler, and one of the sweaty car pushers was on board. The blue-overalled guy was up front, next to Adil. How wrong she'd been, then, in her reading of alliances. Perhaps she might have scored a berth, if she'd pushed. She sipped her Coke thoughtfully as the bakkie pulled away.

Warm Coke: it seemed the electricity had gone too, now.

Lynn picked at the strip of aluminium binding the edge of the table. It could be used for something. In an emergency. She opened a packet of cheese-and-onion chips, surprised by her hunger. She realised she was feeling happy, in a secret, volatile way. It was like bunking school: sitting here where nobody knew her, where no one could find her, on a day cut out of the normal passage of days. Nothing was required of her except to wait. All she wanted to do was sit for another hour, and then another hour after that; at which point she might lie down on the sticky vinyl seat in the tainted sunlight and sleep.

She hadn't eaten a packet of chips for ages. They were excellent. Crunching them up, she felt the salt and fat repairing her headache. Lynn pushed off her sandals, which were hurting, and untucked her shirt. She hadn't dressed for mass evacuation.

The female petrol attendant opened the glass door with a clang, then pushed through the wooden counter-flap. She was a plump, pretty young woman with complexly braided hair. Her skin, Lynn noticed, was clear brown, free from the soot that flecked the motorists. She took a small key on a chain from her bosom and opened the till, whacking the side of her fist against the drawer to jump it out. With a glance across at Lynn, she pulled a handful of fifty-rand notes from the till, then hundreds.

'Taxi's going,' she said.

'Really? With what petrol?'

'He's got petrol. He was just waiting to fill the seats. We made a price – for you too, if you want.'

'You're kidding. He was just waiting for people to pay? He could've taken us any time?'

The woman shrugged, as if to say, taxi drivers. She stroked a thumb across the edge of the wad of notes. 'So?'

Lynn hesitated. 'I'm sure someone will be here soon. The police will come. Rescue services.'

The woman gave a snort and exited the shop, bumping the door open with her hip. The door sucked slowly shut, and then it was quiet again.

Lynn watched through the tinted window as the money was handed over. The transaction revived the inert *gaardjie*. He straightened up and started striding back and forth, clapping his hands, shouting and hustling like it was Main

Road rush hour. The people inside the taxi edged up in the seats and everyone else started pushing in. The driver spotted Lynn through the window and raised his eyebrows, pointing with both forefingers first at her and then at the minibus and then back at her again: coming? When she just smiled, he snapped his fingers and turned his attention elsewhere. People were being made to leave their bags and bundles on the tar.

Lynn realised she was gripping the edge of the table. Her stomach hurt. Getting up this morning, packing her few things, driving all this way ... it seemed impossible for her to start it all again. Decision, action, motion. She wanted to curl up on the seat, put her head down. But the taxi was filling up.

Her body delivered her: all at once, her digestion seemed to have speeded up dramatically. Guts whining, she trotted to the bathroom.

Earlier, there'd been a queue for the toilets, but now the stalls were empty. In the basin mirror, Lynn's face was startlingly grimed. Her hair was greasy, her eyes pink, as if she'd been weeping. Contamination. Sitting on the black plastic toilet seat, she felt the poisons gush out of her. She wiped her face with paper and looked closely at the black specks smeared onto the tissue. Her skin was oozing it. She held the wadded paper to her nose. A faint coppery smell. What *was* this shit? The explosion had been at a chemical plant, but which chemical? She couldn't remember what they'd said on the news.

She noticed the silence. The slightly reverberating stillness of a place that has just been vacated.

There was nobody left on the forecourt. The battered

white taxi was pulling out, everyone crammed inside. The sliding door was open, three men hanging out the side with their fingers hooked into the roof rim. Lynn ran after it onto the highway, but the only person who saw her was the blond toddler crushed against the back windscreen, one hand spread against the glass. He held her gaze as the taxi picked up speed.

The cloud was creeping higher behind her back, casting a murk, not solid enough to be shadow. She could see veils of dirty rain bleeding from its near edge. Earlier, in the city, she had heard sirens, helicopters in the sky; but there was no noise out here.

Standing alone on the highway was unnerving. This was for cars. The road surface was not meant to be touched with hands or feet, to be examined too closely or in stillness. The four lanes were so wide. Even the white lines and the gaps between them were much longer than they appeared from the car: the length of her whole body, were she to lie down in the road. She had to stop herself looking over her shoulder, flinching from invisible cars coming up from behind.

She thought of the people she'd seen so many times on the side of the highway, walking, walking along verges not designed for human passage, covering incomprehensible distances, toiling from one obscure spot to another. Their bent heads dusty, cowed by the iron ring of the horizon. In all her years of driving at speed along highways, Cape Town, Joburg, Durban, she'd never once stopped at a random spot, walked into the veld. Why would she? The highways were tracks through an indecipherable terrain of dun and grey, a blurred world in which one glimpsed only fleetingly the sleepy eyes of people standing on its edge. To leave the car would be to disintegrate, to merge with that shifting world. How far could she walk, anyway, before weakness made her stumble? Before the air thickened into some alien gel, impossible to wade through, to breathe?

It was mid-afternoon but it felt much later. Towards the city, the sky was thick with blood-coloured light. It was possible to stare at the sun – a bleached disk, like the moon of a different planet. The cloud was growing. As she watched, a deep occlusion spread towards her, pulling darkness across the sky. She ducked reflexively and put her hands up against the strange rain. But the raindrops were too big, distinct – and she realised that they were in fact birds, thousands of birds, sprinting away from the mountain. They flew above her and around her ears: swift starlings, labouring geese. Small, rapid birds tossed against the sky, smuts from a burning book.

As they passed overhead, for the first time Lynn was filled with fear.

Approximately fifty packets of potato chips, assorted flavours. Eighty or so chocolate bars, different kinds. Liquorice, wine gums, Smarties. Maybe thirty bottles and cans of Coke and Fanta in the fridges. Water, fizzy and plain: fifteen big bottles, ten small. No alcohol of any kind. How much fluid did you need to drink per day? The women's magazines said two litres. To flush out the toxins. Would drinking Coke be enough? Surely. So: two weeks, maybe three. The survival arithmetic was easy. Two weeks was more than enough time; rescue would come long before then. She felt confident, prepared.

Boldly, she pushed through the wooden flap and went

behind the counter. The till stood open. Beyond were two swing doors with head-high windows, and through them a sterile steel-fitted kitchen, gloomy without overhead lighting. Two hamburger patties, part-cooked, lay abandoned on the grill, and a basket of chips sat in a vat of opaque oil. To the right was a back door with a metal pushbar. She shoved it.

The door swung open on to a sudden patch of domesticity: three or four black bins, a clothesline, sunlight, some scruffy blue-gums and an old two-wire fence with wooden posts holding back the veld. A shed with a tilted corrugated-iron roof leaned up against the back wall. The change in scale and atmosphere was startling. Lynn had not imagined that these big franchised petrol stations hid modest homesteads. She'd had the vague sense that they were modular, shipped out in sections, everything in company colours. Extraneous elements – employees – were presumably spirited away somewhere convenient and invisible at the end of their shifts. But this was clearly somebody's backyard. It smelt of smoke and sweat and dishwater, overlaying the burnt grease of the kitchen. Through the doorway of the shed she could see the end of an iron bed and mattress. On the ground was a red plastic tub of the kind used to wash dishes or babies. Two plastic garden chairs, one missing a leg. A rusted car on bricks.

Lynn laughed out loud. Her car! Her own car, twenty years on: the same model blue Toyota, but stripped to a shell. The remaining patches of crackled paint had faded to the colour of a long-ago summer sky. The roof had rusted clean through in places, and the bottom edges of the doors were rotten with corrosion. Old carpeting was piled on the back seat and all the doors were open. Seeing the smooth finish gone scabrous and raw gave Lynn a twinge at the back of her teeth.

She walked past the car. There was a stringy cow on the other side of the fence, its pelt like mud daubed over the muscles. A goat came avidly up to the wire, watching her with slotted eyes, and she put her arm through and scratched the coarse hair between its horns. The cow also mooched over in an interested way. Smelling its grassy breath, Lynn felt a tremor of adventure. She could be here for *ages*. She felt no fear at the prospect: nobody else was here, nobody for miles around. (Although briefly she saw again: the hand sliding across the throat ...)

Out here, the sky looked completely clear, as if the petrol station marked the limit of the zone of contamination. She shot her fingers at the goat and snapped them like the taxi-man, spun round in a circle, humming.

And breathed in sharply, stepping back hard against the wire. 'Jesus.'

Someone was in the car. The pile of rugs had reconstituted itself into an old lady, sitting on the back seat as if waiting to be chauffeured away.

Lynn coughed out a laugh, slapping her chest. 'Oh god, sorry,' she said. 'You surprised me.'

The old lady worked her gums, staring straight ahead. She wore a faded green button-up dress, a hand-knitted cardigan, elasticised knee stockings and slippers. Grey hair caught in a meagre bun.

Lynn came closer. 'Hello?' she began. Afrikaans? Hers was embarrassingly weak. 'Hallo?' she said again, giving the word a different inflection. Ridiculous.

No response. Poor thing, she thought, someone just left

her here. Would the old lady even know about the explosion? 'Sorry ... *tannie?*' she tried again. She'd never seriously called anyone *tannie* before. But it seemed to have some effect: the old lady looked at her with mild curiosity. Small, filmed black eyes, almost no whites visible. A creased face shrunken onto fine bones. An ancient mouse.

'Hi. I'm Lynn. Sorry to disturb you. Ah, I don't know if anyone's told you – about the accident? In Cape Town.'

The woman's mouth moved in a fumbling way. Lynn bent closer to hear.

'My grandson,' the old lady enunciated, softly but clearly, with a faint smile. Then she looked away, having concluded a piece of necessary small talk.

'He told you about it?'

No answer.

So. Now there was another person to consider, an old frail person, someone in need of her help. Lynn felt her heaviness return. '*Tannie,*' she said – having begun with it she might as well continue – 'There's been an accident, an explosion. There's chemicals in the air. Poison, *gif*. It might be coming this way. I think we should go out front. There might be people coming past who can help us. Cars. Ambulances.'

The old lady seemed not averse to the idea, and allowed Lynn to take her arm and raise her from her seat. Although very light, she leaned hard; Lynn felt she was lugging the woman's entire weight with one arm, like a suitcase. Rather than negotiate the series of doors back through the station, they took the longer route, clockwise around the building on a narrow track that squeezed between the back corner of the garage and the wire fence. Past the ladies, the gents, the café. As they walked, it started to rain, sudden and heavy. The rain shut down the horizon; its sound on the forecourt canopy was loud static. Lynn wondered how tainted the falling water was. She sat the old lady down on a sheltered bench outside the shop, and fetched some bottles of water and packets of chips from inside.

Then she urgently needed to use the bathroom again.

The toilet was no longer flushing. Her empty guts felt liquid, but strained to force anything out. The headache was back.

Outside, she saw the rain had stopped, as abruptly as it started, leaving a rusty tang in the air. The old lady had vanished.

Then Lynn spotted movement out on the road: her car door was open. Coming closer, she saw that the woman was calmly eating tomato chips in the back seat. Having transferred herself from the wreck in the backyard to the superior vehicle out front, she was now waiting for the journey to recommence.

A neat old lady, Lynn noted: there were no crumbs down her front. She seemed restored by the chips. Her eyes gleamed as she whipped a plastic tortoiseshell comb out of a pocket and started snatching back wisps of hair, repinning the bun with those black U-bend pins that Lynn hadn't seen since her own grandmother died.

In contrast, Lynn felt increasingly dishevelled, and embarrassed about her tip of a car: the empty Heineken bottles on the floor, the tissues in the cubbyhole. She should have kept things cleaner, looked after things better.

'My grandson,' the woman said to Lynn, with a nod of reassurance.

'Of course,' said Lynn.

Evening was coming. The clouds had retreated somewhat and were boiling over the mountain. The brief rain had activated an awful odour – like burnt plastic but with a metallic bite, and a whiff of sourness like rotten meat in it too. Lynn sat in the front seat, put the keys into the ignition and gripped the steering wheel. She had no plan. The sky ahead was darkening to a luminous blue. The silent little woman was an expectant presence in her rear-view mirror. Oppressed, Lynn got out of the car again and stood with her hands on her hips, staring east, west, willing sirens, flashing lights. She ducked back into the car. 'I'll be back in a sec, okay? You're all right there?'

The woman looked at her with polite incomprehension.

Lynn just needed to walk around a bit. She headed off towards the sun, which was melting into smears of red and purple. The mountain was no longer visible. The road was discoloured, splattered with lumps of some tarry black precipitate. She counted five small bodies of birds, feathers damp and stuck together. Blades of grass at the side of the road were streaked with black, and the ground seemed to be smoking, a layer of foul steam around her ankles. It got worse the further she walked. She turned around.

There was someone stooped over her car. At once she recognised the moustache, the blue overalls.

Her first impulse was to hide. She stood completely still, watching. He hadn't seen her.

The damp-faced man was holding something … a box. No, a can. He had a white jerrycan in his hands and he was filling her car with petrol. Lynn's stomach roiled and she crouched down at the side of the road, vomiting a small quantity of cheese-and-onion mulch into the stinking grass. When she raised her chin, the man had straightened up, was looking back at the petrol station.

Deciding, she made herself stand, raising her hand to wave. But in that moment he opened the door and got in; the motor turned immediately and the car was rolling forward. She could see the back of the old woman's head, briefly silver as the car turned out into the lane, before the reflection of the sunset blanked the rear windscreen. The Toyota headed out into the clear evening.

Lynn sat in the back of the rusted car and watched the sky turn navy and the stars come out. She loved the way the spaces between the stars had no texture, softer than water; they were pure depth. She sat in the hollow the old lady had worn into the seat, ankles crossed in the space where the handbrake used to be. She sipped Coke; it helped with the nausea.

She'd been here three days and her head felt clear. While there'd been a few bursts of warm rain, the chemical storm had not progressed further down the highway. It seemed the pollution had created its own weather system over the mountain, a knot of ugly cloud. She was washed up on the edge of it, resting her oil-clogged wings on a quiet shore.

Sooner or later, she was certain, rescue would come. The ambulances with flashing lights, the men in luminous vests with equipment and supplies. Or maybe just a stream of people driving back home. But if that took too long, then there was always the black bicycle that she'd found leaned up against the petrol pump. The woman's grandson must have ridden here, with the petrol can, from some place not too far down the road. It was an old postman's bike, heavy but hardy, and she felt sure that if he had cycled the distance, so could she. Maybe tomorrow, or the day after. And when this was all over, she was definitely going to go on a proper detox. Give up all junk food, alcohol. Some time soon.

Lynn snapped open a packet of salt-'n'-vinegar chips. Behind her, the last of the sunset lingered, poison violet and puce, but she didn't turn to look. She wanted to face clear skies, sweet-smelling veld. If she closed her eyes, she might hear a frog, just one, starting its evening song beyond the fence.

ANIMALIA PARADOXA

Île-de-France, 1792

'In Cap d'Afrique,' I tell Michel, 'the cattle are more beautiful than the French varieties. Great spreading horns. Red or grey, or speckled.'

Michel grunts. He watches me with suspicion as I rearrange the bones on the long table in the Countess's orangery.

Through the glass doors and the dome above me, I can see bats flitting in the evening sky. A few lamps burn in the upper rooms of the chateau across the terrace. The Countess is no longer here. After the recent troubles in Paris, she left with her retinue for the countryside, perhaps even for another country. I did not speak with her before she departed. Perhaps I am simply shunned. Perhaps she is seeing other suitors, charlatans selling her the usual curiosities: misshapen bears, dull tableaux of common birds, amusing scenes of mice and foxes.

It is a cool autumn evening, but inside the orangery the

weather is warm, even tropical. For a moment the expanse of glass makes me feel observed, as if I am placed here for display.

Michel is very slow, and has no feeling for the material. He is an ancient village soul, accustomed to the creatures of the old world. He knows how they are put together: four feet, two horns, milk below.

'This cannot be one animal,' he says. He is laying out the long-bones, and indeed there seem to be too many of them, and oddly sized. Everything is in a sorry state. Some of the more delicate items have crumbled to dust in the sea-chests. 'Linnaeus himself does not account for all the creatures of the world,' I tell him. 'Not of Africa.'

Michel lets a femur clatter to the table. 'Monsieur,' he says. 'I am leaving now. You should go too: it is not safe.'

But I cannot go, of course I cannot, not when I am so close. Late at night in the lamplit orangery I work on, fitting femur to radius, long bones to small. Boldness, I think, boldness and vision are needed here. But the bones will not do my bidding. They do not match up. They do not create a possible animal.

The streaks of light fade from the sky; it is that slow cooling of the day, so different to nightfall in southern climes.

I miss the boy's quick hands, quick eyes.

I remember the shape of his head. Jacques, Jakkals. He was a thin child, dressed in nothing but ragged sailor's trousers, held up by twine and rolled to the knee. Hard-soled feet, skin tight over ribs and shoulder-blades. All of him shades of earth and ochre, but flashed with white, like the belly of a springbok as it leaps away. Ostrich-eggshell beads at his neck, teeth like Sèvres porcelain. And that round head, close-shorn. One could imagine the bone beneath. When I first saw him, tagging behind as our party struck north from the Cape, I thought: there are men in France who would like that cranium in their collection. A pretty piece to cup in the palm.

Shadows gutter on the ceiling as the last of the lamp-oil runs out. Outside I see points of light and at first I think they are stars, burning low to the ground: the sky turned upside down. But no. They are flames, moving up the hill from the village, torches lighting faces in the crowd. The voices build.

The last time I saw Jacques his skull was crushed on one side, the front teeth gone, face caked with blood and dust.

I imagine he was buried with the usual native rites. Sitting upright, as I have heard it is done, in the old hide blanket, with nothing to mark the place but a small pile of stones. The vitreous black stones you find there in the north, in that dry country.

Cape of Good Hope

Venter was a chancer from the start. I met him on the church square; he was selling skins and ivory. With what was left of the Countess's money, I was procuring oxen, muskets, what men I could afford.

'I hear you're coming north,' the Boer said, his face shadowed by a leather brim. 'I hear you're looking for animals.'

'Special animals,' I nodded. 'Rare ones.' I had been in the Cape a month by then, and my own rough Dutch was improving.

'Visit with us,' he said. 'We have a hell of an animal for you.'

'Ah. And what kind might that be?'

I was not overly excited. Already I had received several offers of specimens. There had been enough European adventurers in these parts for the locals to imagine they knew what we sought. On the docks, a hunter had thrust a brace of speckled fowl at me, their bodies stinking in the heat. In a tavern, a wrinkled prospector had produced a pink crystal, its facets glinting in the candlelight. But the Countess wished for something she had not seen before. The foot of a rhinoceros, a pretty shell — these would not be enough. One of the slave-dealers had promised more exotic sights, native girls with curious anatomies, but this, too, I had refused. I was looking for something spectacular, something to cause a sensation; but not of that kind.

'It's big,' said Venter.

'Like an elephant? An ostrich?' I said. 'Perhaps a whale?'

'All of those things,' he said, and tilted his head so that his pale eyes caught the sun, colour piercing the hues of hide and roughspun cloth. He was a handsome man, tall and with a strong jaw under his yellow beard, grown very full as is the habit of the farmers here. 'It's all of those things, God help us.'

I tried not to smile at his ignorance. 'Come now, it must be one thing or the other. Fish or fowl.'

He shrugged. 'It flies, it runs. Here,' he said, leaning forward and pulling off his hat. A waft of sweat, a herbal tang, the coppery hair compressed in a ring. 'That is its skin.'

I did not wish to touch the greasy hat, but he pushed it into my hands, pointing at the hide band. Spotted, greyish yellow. It might have been hyena fur, or harbour rat for all I knew.

'Keep it.' He spat his tobacco into the dust. 'You are welcome on my land. Ask for Venter. Up north the people know me.'

It took me several weeks to gather what I needed for the expedition: oxen, two wagons, a donkey, the firelocks, the powder and lead. I could not afford slaves in the end, but employed ten bearers of the race they call here Hottentotten. The arsenical paste for the preservation of the specimens I had brought with me on the ship from France. My collecting trunk, which fitted perfectly into the back of the larger wagon, was a gift from the Countess, made by her own cabinet-maker, and had her initials inlaid in brass on the lid. Inside were dozens of ingenious drawers and racks for glass jars and flasks. I had also with me my fine brass compass — although the little hinged sundial did not work as it should, down in the south — and my most prized possession: my copy of *Systema Naturae*.

The donkey I disliked. It looked exactly like any donkey in any part of France, and was every bit as doltish and mutinous. But the oxen were splendid animals. I was glad to see the mountain growing smaller over their lurching shoulders as our party took the coastal track to the north. Happy to be away from that town, with its hot winds, its slave-drivers from every filthy corner of the world, its rumours of plague and war.

We turned inland. Game was plentiful and we did not lack for meat. It lifted my heart, to be out on those grasslands, with no sounds but the steady hoofbeats of the oxen, the wagons' creak and the good-humoured talk of the men in a language I did not know. Clucks and kisses in it, impossible for my mouth to shape. At times people appeared out of the bush to meet us on the road, and spoke to the men in their own tongue, perhaps asking news of the Cape. As we travelled further north, the land became dryer, flatter, broken by pans of salty mud cracked in honeycomb patterns and pink with roosting flamingos; elsewhere by tumbled piles of glassy black and olive rock. It was wild country. I had high hopes of finding some striped or spotted beast for my lady yet. Indeed, one night we heard a throaty rumble from beyond the firelight. Lion, the men whispered. But it did not approach.

The bearers were easy company. The boy, in particular, was useful; he brought back small animals and interesting pebbles, bird's-nests, snakeskins. As we travelled, he was constantly darting into gullies or turning over stones to gather up a feather, a piece of wool, a beetle carapace. Nothing extraordinary, but I saw that he understood my purpose. When we board-mounted a little bat, he very neatly fanned the wing for me to tap the brass tacks in, without needing instruction. It was hard to tell his age, seventeen or eleven, he was so thin. I think he ate better with me than he ever had in the town. Where he came from, I was not sure. He was not one I hired myself, but seemed to have come along with the older men. Jakkals, they called him. Though that was not his true name, I think. I started to call him Jacques, privately, when we worked on the specimens together. A sentimental impulse: it was the name of my own little boy, lost now these twenty years. With the men I called him Boy.

Some days into our journey, we were passed by a group of riders, also heading north. The commando, as such posses are called, were after a baster gang: thieves and runaways, they said, causing havoc on the farms. A rough bunch themselves, these vigilantes, guns slung across their backs. They peered at our party with suspicion — it was not usual to a see a solitary white gentleman in those parts, certainly not a Frenchman. I mustered my best kitchen Dutch to persuade them on their way.

The commando disturbed my men. After the riders left, kicking up dust to the horizon, they murmured uneasily to each other.

Later, I asked the men about Venter's beast, and handed the hat around the fire. They went silent. Between puffs on their long clay pipes, they said the name of the animal. *Gumma, gauma, gomerah*. Rasped in the back of the throat, in a way I am incapable of reproducing.

'So it is real?'

Hums of assent.

'What does it look like?'

'It has wings, very long.' One man held out his arms. 'Black feathers.'

'And a head like a lizard, with lion's teeth.'

'Very dangerous.'

'It can eat forty, fifty sheep.'

The oldest of the men, a greybeard to whom the others deferred, pushed tobacco into the bowl of his pipe and said in his cracked voice: 'It will look at you. It has the eyes of a man.'

I smiled, to show I did not mind, that they made fun of me in this manner.

The hat was passed to the boy. He did not usually speak in front of the older men, but now he touched the hatband with the tips of his fingers. 'Ghimmra.' He said the name differently, with an altered emphasis, and when they heard him the others grunted and nodded approvingly.

'I know this,' said the boy. 'It is from my place. I am from that place.'

Yes, I thought, that may well be. He has the look of a Bushman child. I wondered how he had come to be in the town.

The quiet authority in his voice, and the gravity of all the men, made me think that perhaps there was truth in Venter's story. This was, after all, a new world. Things were different here. Animals may yet exist of which Linnaeus had no knowledge, I mused. Look at the wonders they have found in New Holland: beasts with both fur and eggs.

The commando was already encamped when we got to Venter's homestead. Not much of a farm at all, just a poor dry tract of stones and sand and a mud cottage. No wife, no children. Some way behind the hovel was a domed skin hut where Venter, it seemed, kept a native woman. The riders were gathered at a fire on the packed earth before the house, drinking brandy; the woman brought them a new cask when the old ran dry. My men made camp some distance away, but I accepted a dram of the harsh white liquor and talked for a while with Venter and his companions.

'So, Mijnheer,' I said to Venter, 'where do you keep this animal you speak of? This – is it right? Geema, geemera.'

He looked at me a little oddly then. 'Where did you learn this name?'

I smiled. 'I am a naturalist, my friend. My task is to learn such things.'

'Come,' he said, quite drunk already and putting an arm around my neck. 'I will show you the proof of it.'

Venter drew me warmly into his tiny house. There was almost no furniture in the single room, just a chair and a bed covered in skins. On top of a wooden trunk sat a weighty old Bible. He set this aside and opened the lid of the chest, then proceeded to bring his precious items out into the lamplight, one by one.

I very nearly laughed out loud. Nothing but ratty pelts and dried-out bones, drawn from a dozen different carcasses. He held up the butchered wing of vulture, then what seemed to be the skull of a large bovid. At least he had not gone to the trouble of stitching it all together into a single beast, as I have seen done in fairground wonder-shows. I would not have been surprised if the man drew out a bolt of flowered cotton cloth and tried to tell me it was the hide of some fearsome predator.

'Sjeemera,' he said. His way of saying the word was different, more sibilant.

I smiled and thanked him and said that this was all most interesting, and that I would be glad to inspect his collection more carefully in the daylight. So as not to offend him, I picked out one or two small items — a few dark quills, a shed snake-skin. If I wanted the bones, he intimated, I would have to pay. I quickly made my goodnights.

I left the fire and the drinking, choosing rather to lie in my own tent, close to the soft snorting and warmth of the oxen. Still, I could hear the men of the commando talking and laughing late into the night.

Jacques, who slept at my feet inside the tent, spoke into the dark: 'The animal, Mijnheer.'

'Yes?'

'I can take you to its place. I know where is its cave.'

I was silent for moment. 'Is it near? Can we walk?'

'No. It is still a day from here. We must take the wagons. We should go tomorrow, early.'

'How do you know?'

'This is my place. My people are here.'

That night there was a great storm, wind lashing the tent, the oxen bellowing. Something shrieked like a child in the trees down near the river. Later, we heard the calls of some large animal – but with a yelping, yawning quality, quite unlike a lion's.

I covered my head with an oily sheepskin kaross and thought of France, the motionless winter trees, the pale light touching the branches as delicately as gilt on the curlicues of the Countess's cabinet of marvels.

In her reception room, I had sat balanced on the spindliest of chairs as she showed me her celebrated collection: birds' nests, curious stones and the skeletons of small animals, arranged in their specially built case of bevelled glass and ornate wood, all lacquered white. Light spattered off the touches of gold leaf, off the sunburst wings of the suspended hummingbirds. A thoroughly unsystematic approach, I noted, *Mammalia* mixed in with *Aves* mixed in with *Fossilia*.

'Is it not pretty?' she asked.

'Indeed, very pretty,' I agreed. High in her powdered hair, among the silken bows, another iridescent hummingbird was pinned. The blue flattered her eyes.

She noticed my gaze and touched the stiff little bird. 'From India,' she said. 'Do they have such things in Afrique?'

'If so, I shall endeavour to discover them, Madame.'

'Hm. I think not,' she said. 'From Afrique I want something … magnificent. A new kind of elephant?'

'Perhaps something not quite so large …'

'A tiger!'

'I believe they lack the striped kind there. I will try for spots.'

'Oh but I like the stripes. In the Jardin du Roi they have a leaping tiger, suspended in the air. It is quite wonderful. See what you can do.'

'Madame.'

That had been months before, but it felt like a hundred years. My mission now seemed laughable. How could the Countess have thought that a spun-sugar cabinet might contain any part of this elemental land? In my half-asleep state, it came to me that I had done things altogether back to front. All her pretty shells and pebbles … I should have put them in my pockets, brought them with me on the ship. And then set them free, here in this world of ancient stones and long horizons.

In the blue dawn, the oxen stood shifting and blowing steam. The men packed the wagons quickly and quietly. It seemed important to leave before the commando stirred from their drunken sleep, although no doubt that would break all this country's laws of hospitality. The armed company had made us nervous, and even the oxen seemed to tread softly for fear of breaking the chill and fragile silence.

I was pleased when the little grey house dipped out of sight as the ground rose, as earlier I had been pleased to leave the town behind. As I had been glad to leave France, too, if I were honest, the dark wave sinking the shore in our wake. Always onwards, to new things. Away from old sadness. New wonders, I told myself.

We found ourselves creaking up the start of a long mountain pass marked by stones. As the wagons ascended and the broad, brightening plain fell away below us, so too my spirits lifted. The track was edged with tiny white and yellow flowers. I thought about collecting them to press, but I did not want to halt our progress. And *Regnum Vegetabile* had never delighted me quite like *Regnum Animale*.

At length we came out onto the neck of the pass, where Jacques indicated we should outspan. Above us was a rough tower of boulders.

'Here,' said Jacques, and started up the scree. He went lightly, leaping barefoot from rock to rock. I struggled behind, sweat soaking my linen shirt. My face was flaming, even shaded by Venter's odorous hat. Below us, the men set about making camp.

In the shade beneath the rocks, the sand was cool. I took a moment to catch my breath. Jacques was crouched close to the base of a boulder, peering at something. At first I could not make it out, but then I saw: an image painted on the stone, about two hands tall. An upright red body with a long pale face like a deer's or a hare's, but the finely muscled legs of a running man. Tiny white dots on the torso.

Despite my flush, I felt myself grow cold. 'Is this what you have brought me to see, this ... hocus pocus?'

He patted the floor of the cave. Was he smiling? The white

sand was scuffed with a multitude of indistinct tracks, including our own. 'Here,' he said. 'Here is where it puts its eggs.'

'But this is no real beast,' I said, angry. I felt more deceived by this primitive display than by Venter's skulduggery. 'This is nonsense, Jacques! Why do you wish to trick me too?'

He did not answer. Instead he squatted and pushed his fingers into the sand, digging away several inches. Under the top layer the soil became damper, darker. A smooth white curve emerged. For a moment I thought it was a human skull, but he shovelled his hands down around it and, after some heaving, forced a gigantic egg to rise from the ground. It was bigger than his head, much bigger than an ostrich egg. When I bent to help him raise it, I felt its weight. It was smooth and cool to the touch, and very heavy, as if full of molten metal. I took my water-skin and poured a little out; washed free of sand, the egg glowed like a great pearl, with a bluish cast.

'What is it, Jacques? What kind of bird?' He spoke quickly, tongue clicking. 'What? I cannot understand.'

He sighed and closed his eyes and his arms floated upwards. Then his head jerked back as if in a fit, ribs jutting tautly. I stopped forward in alarm, then realised: it was a pantomime. This was for me, so I could see the nature of the animal. His hands flapped and slapped his sides. Feet scuffed the sand, tracing a circle. He bowed his neck and kicked at the ground, arms out like wings, then opened his mouth very wide and groaned. Teeth like the white quartz in the rocks, not porcelain at all. Teeth bared as if in pain.

'That's enough.'

At once he stood quite still, as if I had slapped him. I ran my hands over the slick surface of the egg. 'Tell me truthfully, now. Is this creature real?'

The boy nodded, although his eyes were cool.

'Then find me one. Find me one to shoot for my Countess. I have not time for make-believe.'

I wrapped the egg in a piece of oilcloth and put it into my leather bag. Its weight hung awkwardly off my shoulder. As we walked back down the scree slope, I saw below me the two small wagons, the men lounging in the shade. It occurred to me for the first time that they might easily drive off without me, as I had heard happen to other adventurers. Once this thought had struck, it became harder to look away. I felt I needed to pin the men in place with my eyes. I thought of their uneasiness these last days, their murmurings to each other. The boy, I thought; they would not leave the boy behind. But perhaps the boy plans to flee, too. This is where he comes from, these hills.

The men greeted me civilly, but distrust had entered my heart. I sensed their alertness when they saw I carried a prize. The old man came up to me quite boldly, reaching out a hand as if to touch my bag, but I turned away from him, holding it closed.

I laid it next to my camp bed, where I curled up almost immediately, exhausted from the climb. Falling into slumber beneath the odorous kaross, I felt, for the first time on this journey, a longing for home, for walls around me, for the close skies and low ceilings and mossy damp enclosures of the old country. Rather than this bleak kingdom of stones, this *Regnum Lapideum*, roamed by unnameable animals.

The bright sky woke me like a slap. Blue, so blue, it filled my eyes to the edges and beyond. I lay staring up at it for some minutes before I realised what it meant. The tent was gone.

They had taken the horse, the oxen, the wagons, the muskets and ammunition. And Jacques, Jakkals, the boy: gone too.

Leaving me what? The donkey, presumably out of some chivalrous impulse: I could ride it in shame back to Venter's. The egg: it perched on the sand, balanced on one end. They had not wished to take it with them. And my collecting trunk. It stood askew on the ground, spilling its drawers into the sand, preserving fluid leaking from a corner. Its tiny compartments lay open to the sky, its intricate systems mocked by the boundless land. Carefully, I slid the drawers home, checking for broken jars and vials. Of course I could not move it on my own.

At my feet, the dry mud was cracked into hexagons, marked only by the points where the tent-pegs had been sunk, the impress of the cooking pots, the cold firepit and the long churned wake of the oxen. I put on Venter's hat with its fancy band and stood in the small puddle of my own shade.

I would have stayed there perhaps indefinitely, staring at the donkey staring at me, if there had not come some time later — I cannot say how long — the reports of many hooves on the dry earth. It was Venter and the riders. They slowed as they came alongside, and the man nodded a greeting. He seemed amused, hair glinting in the sun as he doffed his new hat. The others barely looked at me; they preferred to read the story directly from the earth. It was not a difficult tale.

The men wheeled their horses around me and took off to the north, faster now, chased by their shadows. That was what the commando was there to do, after all: pursue miscreants, thieves, absconders.

I followed on foot to the top of the pass, where the land fell away. I saw where the wagon wheels had gouged a track, a steep descent back and forth to the plain far below. It was even vaster than the one we had crossed the day before, pale yellow like a scarred old lion-skin, sparsely veined where darker bush marked the watercourses. Far off were flecks of white and gold: a herd of springboks. Their heads were raised at identical angles to watch the slowly fleeing wagons, which churned in their wake a creamy plume of dust that hung in the air like blood in water. My runaway men were heading for a line of pale-blue hills. They did not seem to have gone very far, although the distances were so great it was hard to judge.

Directly below me, more dust rose, marking the far faster progress of the commando. The riders had reached the bottom of the pass and were striking out across the plain. As the two trails converged, I realised that, despite my losses, it was the wagons I was urging on. But the riders were remorseless. A few minutes later, I heard the dull concussion of the first shots. In the long-echoing stillness of the desert air, the buck leaped into the air and away, hanging for a moment on each bound like low-flying birds.

I turned away and walked back to the immobile donkey. I stared up at the blue sky, letting Venter's hat fall from my head. Very high up, a large bird was wheeling, but I could not make out its markings. I could not identify it at all.

In the evening, they found me waiting back at the house. Venter let the boy's body tumble from the back of the horse onto the ground. So light it barely stirred the dust. So blood-ied that at first I thought an animal had slain him. But then I saw his head. Musket-ball, I thought. I'd seen that kind of wound many years ago, a boy myself, in the Spanish wars.

'We lost the others in the hills,' Venter said, shouldering past me into the house. The stench of powder and sweat and blood. 'Godverdomme. Brandy.'

Outside in the raw sun, I saw the kitchen woman come, not with brandy but with an old kaross in her hands, dark and creased as a tobacco leaf. She knelt to fold it around the boy's body, tucking it close with tense thrusts that made the muscles stand on her lean arms. At the last, he looked like a seed in a pod, a bat wrapped in its wings for the night.

South Atlantic Ocean

Already on the ship I could tell the specimens were rotting, that my techniques for preservation had failed in some or all of them. Perhaps the dank air in the hold had affected the formula, or seawater breached the wax seals. Not trusting the seamen with the delicate objects, I had chosen to keep them in the cabin with me. I lie on top of my trunks like a dragon on its hoard. I found it kept the seasickness at bay, despite the smells of meat and arsenic, to press my cheek to the cool wood. I dreamed the sea-chest beneath me was a cof-fin lid, with beneath it Jacques' face, lips drawn back from broken teeth. But Jacques was buried under stones, hands clutched around his ankles. Far from the sea.

The trunks were my fortune. I'd bartered every other thing I owned to get that damned Boer to haul me and my cases and jars back to the Cape with its hellish summer winds. With every mile my monies bled away. The oxen, the guns and the wagons, the servants ... all those seemed now like outrageous riches, as opulent as the Countess's silver dinner service.

I'd even sold Venter my precious *Systema*. He had put it next the Bible on his chest carved of yellow wood. I doubt very much the man could read either book. But it comforted me that Linnaeus's pages were not blowing through the veld, catching on thorns, being used to light pipes around camp-fires. At the last, the scoundrel pressed his piteous collection of pelts and bones upon me; that at least was something.

Neuroptera, Mineræ, Muraena, I breathed through my nausea. If I turned my head towards the blue porthole, I might glimpse a long head turned towards me, obscured by the slow flap of a leathery wing, riding the hot wind from the Cape. At other times, the creature followed beneath the ship. Once, in the early morning, I heard a deep boom shiver through the body of the vessel and I knew: it was pounding its head against the keel.

But when I went on board later that day, the men explained: 'Cannonballs. Did you not realise? But we are safe now, by God's grace.'

Corsairs. I laughed, and the sailors looked at me strangely.

In my notebook I tried to scratch a sketch of the creature I saw in my dreams, its serpent neck, its gaping jaws. *Amphibia, Vermes, Hydra.* The words were fading from my mind. The pen skittered away from me, the inkpot spilled.

In the third week at sea, the captain, a melancholy Swede, red-eyed, came down to complain of the smell, and insisted that the skins be turfed over the side. I was too sick to resist. Each drawer of my wooden cabinet was filled with corruption and shame: all lost, all for nothing.

But still I had the bones, and the egg in its wool-packed box. If I pulled aside the wool and laid my finger on the shell, I fancied I could feel some movement, a flip or shift in the sac of fluid within. Could it be alive? One storm-rocked night it escaped its nest and rolled elliptically across the deck. I scrambled after it, trapping it with my body.

At times I thought: this will be the making of me. It will be a sensation.

At other times I thought: it is my ruination.

Île-de-France

I have given up on the bones. All I have left is the bluish egg, heavy as a cannonball. It was cool when we found it, but here in the orangery I can feel it has gained warmth, like a quickening thing. Palms pressed to its curve, I close my eyes; the last thing I see in the gloom is the egg's pale glow, like seashells, like bone, like quartz. I try to remember the shape of the painted creature on the rock, those many months ago. The red flanks, the calves and thighs, the long muzzle. The sheen of the wet rock behind it. A wonder.

Outside, shouts and the sound of breaking glass. The windows of the chateau. I think of the famous white cabinet, rocking on its ball-and-claws. The mob is coming closer, *Vive la Révolution*, and now the egg trembles against me as if in answer to that roar. Flames on my eyelids, an orange campfire light.

Breaking glass again, and closer, and all around. A wrench inside the shell. A black blast, a roar of heat: shards of glass strike me and as I topple back I feel the great egg crack in my arms, and something blood-hot and wet and writhing clambers from my grasp. As the walls of the orangery shatter around me, the newborn opens its wings.

When I wake I am on my back, staring up at the dark sky. The dome is broken. The chateau burns, and orange-lit smoke obscures the stars. It is too late for fear.

High above, the great forms hangs with wings outspread. Lizard-jawed, fish-scaled, coal-feathered, impossible. It pulls back its neck and screams. I cry out: something wordless, for it has no names that I can say.

It hears.

Looping its serpentine body, it turns and drops towards me. A hot rush of wind, and for a moment I see its giant eye.

It is a human eye, and every other kind besides. It is like no living thing, and yet contains all living things. It is animal and mineral and angel, and every being yet to be invented, all creatures of the coming age.

It rises up again, on wings of smoke and fire.

ACKNOWLEDGEMENTS

Warmest thanks to Boiler House Press: Philip Langeskov and Jasmin Kirkbride for their sensitive editing, Nathan Hamilton, designer Emily Benton, cover artist Kristy Campbell, and everyone involved in making this beautiful book.

Immense gratitude as always to my agent, Isobel Dixon.

I am indebted to the institutions that supported me while writing these stories: Akademie Schloss Solitude, the Caine Prize for African Writing, Kunst:raum Sylt Quelle Foundation, The National Research Foundation of South Africa, South African PEN, the University of East Anglia, the Gordon Institute for Performing and Creative Arts (University of Cape Town).

And to everyone who read and helped me with these stories over the years, especially: Fourie Botha, Darrel Bristow-Bovey, JM Coetzee, Peter Colenso, Isobel Dixon, Martha Evans, Jarred McGinnis, Jean McNeil, Willam Pierce, Dani Redd, Eustacia Riley, Olivia Rose-Innes, Jared Shurin, Ivan Vladislavić.

Stories in *Animalia Paradoxa* originally appeared in the following publications: 'Sanctuary': *The BBC International Short Story Award 2012*, Comma Press, 2012. 'The Second Law': Galley Beggar Press, 2017. 'Promenade': *Touch*, Zebra Press, 2009. 'The Leopard Trap': *Carrying the Universe*, Eulitz Productions, 2007. 'Limerence': Somesuch Stories, 2016. 'The Boulder': *Jambula Tree and Other Stories: the Caine Prize for African Writing 8th Annual Collection*, Jacana / New Internationalist, 2008. 'Homing': *Homing*, Umuzi / Penguin Random House, 2010. 'Porcelain': *180 Degrees,* Oshun Books, 2005. 'Star': *Elf: Fußballgeschichten aus Südafrika*, ed. Manfred Loimeier, Peter Hammer Verlag, 2010. 'Poison': *African Pens: New Writing from Southern Africa*, Spearhead Press / New Africa Books, 2007. 'Animalia Paradoxa': *Irregularity*, Jurassic London, 2014. 'The Bronze Age': *The Extinction Event*, Jurassic London, 2016.

All stories have been re-edited for this collection.

A*nimalia Paradoxa*
By Henrietta Rose-Innes

First published in this edition by Boiler House Press, 2019
Part of UEA Publishing Project
Copyright © Henrietta Rose-Innes, 2019

The right of Henrietta Rose-Innes to be identified as the Author
of this work has been asserted by her in accordance with the
Copyright, Design & Patents Act, 1988.

Design and typesetting by Emily Benton Book Design
Typeset in Arnhem Pro
Printed by Tallinn Book Printers
Distributed by NBN International

ISBN 978-1-911343-56-1